Murder makes a Mistake

CHARMAIN Z. BRACKETT

DIAMOND KEY PRESS

Published October 2020

Cover art by Ashlee Henry

Dedication

In 2022, I updated my original dedication.

Usually, this is the spot where I say that all the characters are fictional. Any resemblance to anyone, living or dead, is purely coincidental. And that's true except for a couple of characters. One of my characters is based on a composite of journalists I've had the privilege of working with over the course of 30-plus years. I used the radio format for Robert Parnell because of the dramatic effect. The character is mostly based on the print journalists I know. They've written the hard stories and confronted people when necessary. They aren't perfect, but they have worked to get the story right every time they've written or broadcasted one. Journalists are humans. They do make mistakes, but the people I've had the honor of working with, never maliciously reported anything. And their work has made a difference.

I'd like to mention Rob Pavey, with whom I had the privilege of working early in my career in the Columbia County Bureau of The Augusta Chronicle. Rob is one of those people I emulated. Without him and his research, a killer would've gotten away with cold-blooded pre-meditated murder. A year after the case of a man who murdered his wife and adopted son had gone cold, Rob wrote an article with extensive research. The man was arrested soon after Rob's story broke. The husband and father was convicted and executed for the double murder. I'm honored to have been able to have learned just a few things from Rob.

Many others at The Augusta Chronicle and later in my time as managing editor at The Augusta Press have molded this dedication to my fellow journalists. They've also influenced the journalist I am today. Their constant infusion of knowledge made me realize I was up

Book 5 in the Grace's Augusta Mystery Series is Murder Takes A Bow.
https://www.amazon.com/dp/B07ZCB9J1R

for the task when I didn't think I was. I'd like to thank Scott Hudson for believing in me.

Thank you to all of you and the work you do. And last but not least, there is a nod to Grace's family tree, but it's really the author's family tree because there's a piece of me in Grace. Thanks also to Historic Augusta for the historic preservation work you'd done in Augusta, and thanks for the Walk with the Spirits tour. It's a lot of fun. Thank you, Jerry Murphy, who made my Grace moment at Magnolia Cemetery surreal.

1

"Grace, what on earth are you doing?"

Trevor had walked into the kitchen. Most of the people who came over to his home after Mrs. Blake's funeral had already left. I'd hidden in the kitchen, busying myself by loading the dishwasher, wiping off counter tops, and rearranging his refrigerator to put in as many casseroles as possible. I'd felt like an interloper through most of the whole process. Over the past eight weeks, he and I had re-developed our deep friendship not a romantic relationship like everyone I knew in Augusta thought.

I wasn't going to pursue any kind of relationship while I was still married to Drew, even if it was in name only. I wouldn't cheat on him even though he'd made it abundantly clear he didn't want me in his life, and we weren't in contact at all. He gave me money to pay the mortgage the two months he'd been gone. He'd agreed to do that. It was through an electronic transfer, so I didn't have to see him. Still everything hurt. It was the worst emotional pain I'd ever felt, and sometimes the emotional pain was so strong, my body ached.

I'd started calling Mrs. Blake, "Miss Harper." She had wanted me to call her by her first name of "Harper," but I just couldn't. It was one of those Southern respect kinds of things, calling a woman by her first name but giving her a courtesy title. All my life, I'd done this with my mom's friends and some of the older ladies at church. It wasn't as formal, but I still could be respectful.

At Miss Harper's viewing and funeral, I felt like people were staring and talking about Trevor and me. He kept me close by his side at the viewing, and he insisted I sit with the family at the funeral. It was awkward, but because he'd asked, I agreed. I felt like the wanton married woman, but nothing was further from the truth.

What was true was that I visited Trevor's house almost every day as his mother's cancer took its destructive course. He sat with her most of the time I was there. I listened to him talk to her. He was such a good son. He read to her and sang to her. He was completely devoted. And when she slept, which was a lot especially toward the end, we talked, and we cooked, and I started falling back in love with him. And I was sure he felt the same. There was nothing physical between us. He had become my best friend; well besides Emmie and Beth, of course.

In Georgia, it's easy to get a divorce. You can even do-it-yourself with the right forms that you can download from the Internet, which is what Drew did. I'll never forget the last times I saw him. He had visited the treatment facility in North Carolina, but he didn't stay. He'd left with my brother on a Saturday, but on Monday, he was in my shop, wanting to know what I'd done with the divorce papers he'd left me. When I told him I'd shredded them, he got angry with me again. So much for things being left up to me as he claimed they would be. I signed his papers, and he filed them quickly. I think he had someone pull some strings because we were in front of a judge by the end of the week. Once we went before a judge and agreed to terms, that was it. From the time you file to the time it's final can be a measly 31 days. And then, you get a letter in the mail telling you it's finished – an official letter! Miss Harper had been in the hospital the week we filed so Trevor didn't know it had been done. Beth did. She'd finally returned from her travels, and I asked her to watch my shop while I went to court with Drew. I rarely leave my shop, so she knew it had to be important. I begged her not to say anything to anyone. She was a paradox. She knew all the gossip, but she could still keep a secret, especially an important one. She liked to play shop keeper, so I agreed that she could do it on a more regular basis. I guess that was her form of blackmail.

It was turning out to be a horrible holiday season. Miss Harper had died. And then the day before her funeral, just days away from what would've been my 11th wedding anniversary, my letter showed up, notifying me that my divorce was final. That only added to my tears at her funeral. It rained that day, making her funeral exceptionally dreary.

I'd always loved Christmas. That's why I'd chosen a December wedding date. The flowers at Christmas, the red and white poinsettias, carnations, and roses combined with the holly and the fir trees had a magical sort of beauty. All of that made for the best wedding décor.

This year, I wanted to skip all the festivities. There were plenty of beautiful weddings during the holiday season, and I think I cried with every arrangement. I hadn't pulled out the first decoration at my house, but Trevor had tried to make it special for his mother, knowing she probably wouldn't see Christmas. For a while, he came and picked up the flowers for his mother, but as she continued to weaken, he had me deliver them to her. And on those delivery days, he often asked me to stay. We shared some sweet moments such as decorating a gorgeous live tree with her favorite ornaments, and we watched lots of Nutcracker ballets online with her. She and I had gotten close again. Trevor and I would pull chairs up to either side of her bed and each of us would hold one of her hands while we watched the ballet together. It was hardly a romantic relationship.

I made every variation of a Christmas flower arrangement I could think of for her. Her room was filled with the beauty of the season so much red, white, and green. I'd even thrown in some burgundy and gold. Despite the sadness from knowing that she wasn't going to be here much longer, there was a spirit of joy because she seemed to take in every moment and every gift. She amazed me because I knew she was in incredible pain, but she never complained. I tried so hard to put on a brave face. I cried a lot at my shop over the flowers I arranged. I think Trevor knew some of what I was going through, but his mother dying was more important than my failed marriage. I would live despite the pain of my broken heart. He would forever have a hole in his heart when his mother left. He tried to ask me about things with Drew. All I ever told him was that I didn't think he and I would get back together. I tried to leave it at that. I didn't want to give him a timeline. I wasn't sure what he wanted from me, and I didn't think I had it to give anyway. I felt used up and empty except when it came to the flowers. The flowers gave me the love that I could in turn give to Miss Harper and to Trevor.

I was in the middle of wiping down the kitchen counters for the fourth or fifth time when Trevor interrupted my train of thought.

"Grace, what are you doing?" he asked again.

"With so many people coming through here today, I just wanted to put the food away and tidy things up for you, so you didn't have a mess in here."

I was still wearing my black dress, black pumps and pearls from the funeral. I must've looked like a 1950s sitcom mom. I was even wearing an apron. Yes, an apron. I didn't know they still made those, but there was one in the kitchen.

There had been so much food. His sisters-in-law took a lot of it home for their teenage boys. I stayed out of their way. I really felt the glances from them. When they'd left, I made my way into the kitchen. I hid in the background for most of the day. I got a lot of side glances during the funeral, and there was a lot of whispering. Trevor asked me to stay close to him, and I did. I think he was oblivious to all the whispers and stares, but I wasn't. I kept reminding myself I wasn't there for them. I was there for Trevor and his mom.

He walked over to me.

"You're my guest, Grace. Don't worry yourself with that. You know that Mary comes twice a week to help. She'll be here tomorrow, and she can mop the floor. I don't want you doing that in that dress and heels. That's what we pay her to do. I'll even give her extra this week since there have been so many people coming through, and it's

Christmas."

I rinsed out the sponge and placed it on the sink. I turned toward him with my back to the sink, but I stared at the floor. I couldn't look at him. I was on the verge of tears.

"What's the matter?" he asked.

"What do you mean? Your mother just died. It's been a hard couple of months, watching her slip away and now the funeral. I think we're all emotionally spent."

I knew what he was asking, but I didn't want to tell him.

"I know you cared for my mother, but you had more tears than I would've expected. And you're practically scrubbing my kitchen dressed like that. I know that's not what you usually wear to deep clean, is it?"

He smiled at me. He'd moved closer and put his hand on my face to wipe away the stray tears. He tilted my chin, forcing me to stare into his beautiful blue eyes.

"So, I'll ask you again. What's the matter?"

I turned back around to face the sink. I bit my lip, hoping it would stop the tears. I wasn't sure why I ever did that because it never worked. My mind was racing. I tried to think of something to say besides the truth. When nothing came, I blurted it out.

"My divorce has been finalized. I got a letter in the mail yesterday."

He waited for a moment.

"Why didn't you tell me?" he asked softly. He'd moved much closer to me. I could feel his breath on my neck as he whispered in my ear.

"I haven't told anyone."

He touched my arm and moved to my side.

"Grace, look at me," he pleaded gently.

I turned to face him, but I couldn't look him in the eye. I still had so much guilt and shame over the divorce and the fact that people were talking about me and judging me and him too. None of that seemed to bother Trevor in the slightest. I thought I'd moved passed some of these feelings, but they were still there. I knew I still loved Drew in spite of everything that had happened.

"Why didn't you tell me?" he asked again softly, stressing the word "me." "I thought we'd gotten close over these past few weeks."

I looked briefly at him and gave a weak smile.

"Your mother was dying. I wasn't going to be selfish and saddle you with my problems. You didn't need that on top of everything else you were dealing with. When I came over here, I could put that out of my mind. Focusing on you and her was the best thing for me. Nothing was more important to me than making your mother's last days special."

I paused.

"She didn't need depressed people around her. Besides, I haven't even told Emmie or my mother that we even filed. Everyone keeps looking at me like I'm Hester Prynne from The Scarlet Letter. I'm thinking about sewing one on my clothes – the letter "A," that is. After today, I really feel like I need to do that."

"What other people think of us doesn't matter. I know we didn't cross any lines. We didn't have an affair that caused him to leave you. He left before I showed up, not that that is anyone's business anyway."

"I feel like such a failure."

I glanced at the floor when I said that. I had a hard time keeping his gaze. I was afraid of him seeing into me.

"Grace," he said. I turned to look at him. His brow was furrowed as he slowly spoke.

"He forced this on you. You were willing to stick it out even though I believe some of what he did was emotionally abusive. No wife should live in fear of her husband, but you did. I saw how afraid of him you were. You told me things had been difficult between the two of you for almost a year. You did not fail him; he failed you."

There was an angry edge in his voice one I honestly couldn't remember ever hearing.

He was right about the fear and possible emotional abuse. I couldn't call it abuse though. I never thought of Drew as abusive

– not the Drew I'd married. I guess I was afraid of that word, but I had become afraid of my husband right before he walked out on me. It had escalated with Bill Andrews' murder in October. But I guess it had been escalating for months, and I didn't even realize it. He didn't want me helping him on his case. Everything I did set off his anger. His drinking only got worse, and I think – no, I know – it contributed to his anger.

Trevor brushed my cheek with his fingertips. I gazed into his eyes. I could see the concern there.

"I can understand you crying over this. The divorce finalization ripped open the wound that had started healing, but don't cry because you feel like you failed him. He failed you. You have been so concerned about breaking your vows and not committing adultery, but what about the part of marriage vows that include words of love, honor, cherishing your wife? He broke all those. I probably shouldn't talk about him that way, but it seems you think everyone blames you for the break-up. That's simply not the case."

I gave him a weak smile.

"That's sweet of you, but I wasn't perfect."

"You're a human being. Of course, you're not perfect. I haven't met one perfect person yet."

He leaned his head to the side and paused.

"Just so you know, I've spoken to your brother, your parents, and to Beth and Emmie. And to Jazzy, who apparently loves me."

I laughed. Jazzy did love him.

"When did you do all this?"

"It doesn't matter. What matters is that they know what's important for them to know, and that's that I didn't come between the two of you. And I didn't have to tell any of them that. They already knew. They love you, Grace, and they only want you to be happy."

I could feel the tears running down my cheeks, and there was a pause as I looked at him. It was a nervous pause. Standing this close to him, I could feel my heart pounding in my chest. He gently leaned over to kiss my forehead before letting me go. I have no idea what kind of expression was on my face. Being so close to him, I'd thought he might kiss me, but not on the forehead.

He laughed softly.

"I'd much rather kiss you on the lips, but you aren't ready for that," he said as though he could read my mind. He was probably right. I stared at him. I was confused. He was good at reading facial expressions. He told me he'd learned a lot about body language from patients.

"Well, for one thing, you're still wearing these," he said, as he reached out for my left hand and touched my rings.

I pulled my hand away from his and put it behind my back. My engagement and wedding rings weren't expensive, and some might not have even called them pretty. I didn't have a massive solitaire just a few diamond chips in a cluster setting and a thin golden band, but they were mine. Drew was a deputy when he proposed. It wasn't like he made enough money to buy me anything fancy. I glanced away from Trevor. I was embarrassed. I guessed I should've taken them off by now. Ultimately, I didn't want to believe it was over.

"I hardly ever took them off when we were married. I feel like they're part of me."

"You and he were married for a long time."

I nodded sadly.

"Our 11th anniversary would've been Sunday. We were together 14 years in all. Three years of dating and…."

With that, I started crying again.

"I'm sorry, Grace."

He brushed my tears away. He pulled me into his arms, holding me close while I cried.

After several moments, I lifted my head. Although he loosened his hands from around my waist, he didn't let me go completely.

"I'm sorry, Trevor."

"Don't be. I'm sorry you're hurting, but I'm not sorry you and he are divorced. It means I have hope for a second chance with you."

He smiled at me. I could only describe it as a kind smile. It made me feel at ease in one way, but at the same time, there were other feelings I didn't know how to deal with just yet. I swallowed. Those flutters I'd felt when he walked into my shop in October were there in full force. I knew that I loved him or at least part of me did. But at the same time there was a wave of negative emotions inside me as he held me close to him. I'd been married to Drew for so long I didn't know how not to be Mrs. Grace Ward. My mind went to Drew. Trevor said that I didn't fail Drew; that it wasn't my fault for the divorce, but Trevor also told me it wasn't my fault that he and I broke up all those years before. What was it about me that caused men to leave me? What if I got into a relationship with Trevor, and he left me again? I didn't think I could do this. I had to stop it before it even started.

"I need to go home," I said, pulling away as the fear flooded my mind.

"What's the matter? Did I say something wrong?"

"Nothing. You didn't do anything," I said. But what I was thinking was that now that the divorce was final, I was so scared. I didn't want to jump into another relationship. What if I screwed it up too?

His face fell. He had an unnerving way of almost reading my mind.

"Both of us are trying to figure out things in our lives right now. I was just hoping we could do it together."

I didn't know what to say. I looked at the floor.

"Grace, do you really want to go home - alone? Now? It's still early."

"No."

He'd never been to my house. He didn't know that I'd sold a majority of my furniture and pared it back because I was going to have to sell it. It needed a few fresh coats of paint, which I couldn't

9

bring myself to do. Drew was paying part of the mortgage until we sold it. I couldn't have done it all on my own. I hated to put it on the market. I loved that little house, and I didn't know where I'd live once it sold. Then it truly would mark the end of my relationship with Drew. We had so many hopes and dreams in that place.

"Then let's go out. We can have dinner or whatever you want."

I had to laugh because of the abundance of food in the refrigerator and freezer. In the South, food is associated with comfort, and funerals brought out the cookbooks and the casserole dishes. Miss Harper had a lot of friends and so did her sons. There were more casseroles at this house than there were at a church anniversary dinner on the grounds.

"I'm not hungry. If you are, there's plenty here to eat. I think you will eat some kind of casserole for the next month."

I tried to laugh, but he looked serious.

"You've lost weight, Grace, not that you needed to. And I've even tried to feed you."

"I just don't have an appetite these days."

He sighed and smiled at me.

"You don't want to eat, and I don't want you to go home alone. What do you want to do?"

"We could drive to Aiken and see the lights at the gardens."

"A walk through romantic lights at night?" he asked and laughed. "Besides, you aren't dressed to walk around outside."

I tried to laugh too. It hurt too much to laugh though.

"I'll go home so I can change."

He smiled.

I went to grab my phone and purse, and I noticed multiple texts and calls from Emmie in the past 30 minutes. I called to see what was so urgent, but instead of her answering, I heard Trevor's doorbell ring. I ended the call. I knew she was at the door. I swallowed hard. I felt a knot form in the pit of my stomach. Over the past few days, I had an uneasy feeling about Drew, and I couldn't shake it. I'd even had a couple of hazy dreams, nothing definite. I knew something was wrong, but I couldn't reach out to him. He didn't want to talk to me. He didn't want to see me, and I couldn't take the rejection.

"It's Emmie," I said, choking out the words.

2

Trevor narrowed his eyes before he left the kitchen. He looked puzzled, and I gave him a weak smile. I knew her coming over meant something bad, and I knew it had to be her at the door. He walked to the front door, and I timidly followed. I didn't want to hear what Emmie had to say.

Sure enough, when he opened the door, Emmie burst through and walked directly to me without saying a word to Trevor. She put one hand on each of my arms and stared at me.

"What happened to Drew?"

Her jaw dropped, and she stared at me.

"How did you -?" she sighed. "Never mind. You obviously haven't been listening to the radio."

"With the funeral - "

"I know, honey. I know, but this is – "

She paused. She opened her mouth as though she was going to say something, but she didn't speak.

"Bad." I finished the sentence.

"Very."

She took a deep breath and turned to Trevor, forgetting about me for a second.

"I'm sorry for barging in here, hon," she said to him without waiting for him to answer.

"Emmie, what's wrong with Drew, and what's on the radio?"

My heart sank as fear rushed over me. She led me to a chair, and she just kept shaking her head at me. I grabbed her arms and looked her in the eye. I could feel tears welling up yet again, but this time for a different reason.

"Just spit it out, or I'll go turn on the radio."

"Drew's been arrested in the suspicious death of a woman."

"Drew – arrested? What are you talking about?"

She glanced away briefly and swallowed.

"Drew has been charged in the death of Vanessa Graham. Grace, I think he was seeing her, or at least, that's what Butch told me."

Seeing her. He was seeing someone. He had killed someone he was dating. I couldn't process this. I stood up. I only knew of one person who'd be talking about this on the radio, and that was Robert Parnell. He had a talk radio show in the late afternoon, early evening. If it happened in Augusta or the surrounding area, he would uncover it. He spent a lot of time on corruption, injustice and just general bad behavior by public officials - and regular people too - but if you were a public official, you'd better behave. He didn't lie, and he didn't make up stuff. He always had the necessary proof to back things up. In the process, he'd made a lot of enemies. I walked into the living room. There was a record player/radio console in the room, a throwback to the 1960s. I turned it on and moved the dial to the station The Parnell In the Afternoon Show was on.

"Here's the deal," I heard him say. "Until now, Drew Ward has had an exemplary record."

My knees got weak, and I steadied myself on the console.

"He's received a lot of citations for his service. He's had a stellar career in his 15-plus years with the department. But the officers I'd talked to said he had been going through a hard time since the death of his friend and fellow officer Mark Collins a year ago in October. If you remember, Collins killed his wife and then himself. Apparently, Ward was the mediator. He was trying to talk Collins down from the ledge. Ward was promoted in April and helped bust that human trafficking ring that was at work during the tournament, if you recall that one. There was some underage stuff going on in there which was not cool, so he did a great public service. And he also infiltrated that Russian diamond smuggling operation that ended with the dead ballerina in May. But the officers also said he had been having some marital problems. His estranged wife, Grace, owns a flower shop in town."

A knife entered my heart when he said, "estranged wife," I never thought I'd be referred to as that, and he said my name on the radio.

"Like I said, I'll have more information when it becomes available, but Richmond County homicide investigator Drew Ward has been arrested in the shooting death of an as yet unnamed victim. The name is being withheld pending notification of next of kin. I'm hearing that voluntary manslaughter charges are being considered. This didn't take place while he was on duty, and details are sketchy at this point."

With that, I felt my knees buckle under me, and a chill went down my entire body. I felt Trevor next to me. He wrapped his arms around me to steady me. This couldn't be happening. Not Drew. They had the wrong person.

I stood up, gently pushing Trevor away. I turned around to see Trevor and Emmie staring at me. I was stunned. I couldn't say anything. I'd known something was wrong, but never would I have thought this. I couldn't believe he was in jail, and he had been seeing someone. Yes, it bothered me that he was seeing someone so soon. I didn't think of my relationship with Trevor as dating.

I walked past Trevor and Emmie without saying anything. I stepped out of my pumps, and I slipped out the back door to the porch. The house was built into the side of a hill, so the main floor was ground level at the front of the house, but toward the back of that floor, the grade was such that there was enough space for another floor to be built below it. A porch wrapped around the back and overlooked the expansive grounds. Despite it being December, the temperatures were moderate. It was in the 60s and wet from the rains.

I walked toward the wicker porch furniture and lowered myself to the seat. I pulled my legs to me and wrapped my arms around them. I could hear my mother's voice telling me it wasn't ladylike, but I didn't care. I just wanted to be left alone to cry. I felt Emmie sit next to me.

"Grace, honey," she said, placing her hand on my arm.

"Emmie, just leave me alone."

"The police are looking for you. They want to talk to you since Drew was – "

She knew. I knew that it would only be a matter of time before everyone knew, but there were some people I wanted to be the one to tell.

"I don't know anything. I haven't seen Drew since – "

My mind went back to that day in the judge's chambers when he and I signed the papers. I didn't look at him the whole time. I couldn't without fear of breaking down. I felt like I was dying inside. We'd agreed to sell the house and split the profits. His name wasn't on my business. In hindsight, I guess that was good. My parents had actually helped me start it, and they had co-signed a few loans to help with the start up. He didn't want any access to it either, even though he did have a key to it for practical reasons. As soon as we finished, I left the room without glancing at him and rushed to my car, so he wouldn't see me crying. He followed me though and got to the car about the same time as I did. He put his hand on my door as if he was trying to stop me from getting in it. It didn't matter. My hands were shaking, and I couldn't get the door opened in time.

"Grace," he'd said as I stood there crying.

I kept my eyes on my car door. I tried not to look at him. I didn't want him to see me that way. I didn't want anyone to see me that way.

"You've got what you wanted, Drew. You should be happy. Just leave me alone." I tried to choke out the tears.

"Gracie, look at me."

Hearing him call me "Gracie" punched me in the chest. Whenever he'd called me by that name, I always thought it meant "I love you" and "I'll take care of you."

I turned to peer at his face. I was surprised to see there were tears in his eyes too.

"I never wanted this," he whispered.

"Then why are you doing this to me?"

"There are things I can't explain right now, and – "

He paused. He glanced away and took a deep breath.

"Gracie, I may need your help."

"You want me to help you?"

It was more of a question than a statement. I was confused. "Drew, I've tried."

"That's not what I mean," he said.

He took a deep breath and looked around.

"I'm working on something I can't tell anyone about. You've helped me solve three murders. I told you you're a better investigator than I am. You just know things sometimes – not everything but enough to ask the right questions. You have great instincts. And you have this knack of being in the right place at the right time. Trust your dreams, Gracie. I know I didn't want to hear about them, but they've been right. Trust your instincts, and when it comes to me, please trust them."

"I don't understand, but Drew, you know I'd do anything for you."

"I know, Grace, and that's what scares me the most. It might get you killed one day. I don't want you to die on my account."

"That's crazy talk."

"I'm just telling you that there are things going on. Dangerous things. I don't know who to trust, but I always know I can trust you. And if anything ever happens to me –"

"Wait a minute. Don't say that."

I felt a chill down my spine as he said that. He reached out for my hand and forced me to look into his eyes.

"If anything ever happens to me, you'll know what to do. I trust you," he said and paused. "And it could be sooner rather than later."

"Drew, you're scaring me."

"I'm sorry, Grace. I feel like the world is closing in on me."

"Then, don't do this. We can work this out."

"I have to, and trust me, I'll only involve you if I exhaust all other options. I want to do this on my own, but –"

"Please tell me what's going on."

"I can't," he said and grimaced. He took a breath. "And I'm so sorry I got angry and accused you of sleeping with Trevor."

I didn't answer. That came out of left field.

"There's nothing going on between us. He's a friend and now he's a customer. He wants flowers for his dying mother. There's nothing going on romantically."

"I know that. This is just better for you that I'm not in your life for so many reasons. I wish I could explain. Maybe I can one day. I'm sorry, Grace."

He leaned over and gave me a peck on the forehead. But he lingered there. I took in a deep breath as tears rolled down my cheeks. Then he turned away from me.

The words "I'm sorry, Grace" rang in my ears.

I remember standing and staring as I watched him walk to his vehicle. He drove away as I stood there crying. That was the last time I saw him. That night when I got home from the shop, all of his belongings were gone, and his house key was on the table. I started sleeping on the couch after that. I wondered if the reason he wanted a divorce so badly was because there was someone else. It would've made sense to me, more sense than the reasons he gave.

"Grace, honey," I heard Emmie's voice.

"Please, Emmie, I can't take anymore today. I still love him."

"You don't need to go to work tomorrow or the rest of the week," she said.

"I have to. It's Christmas, and it's been busy. I've missed

yesterday and today."

"Beth is more than capable, and you know it. You know she will jump in feet first. Jazzy is on Christmas break from school, and I have a couple of days that I can go in too. The FBI contract extension was only part time and temporary."

"Thanks, Emmie, but – "

"No buts, sweetie. The press will have a field day with this, and you're his wife. They already know who you are, and they will want to talk to you. Who knows – Robert Parnell could be looking for you. They could show up at your house. The only people you need to talk to are the police. Also, you probably don't want to go home right now. The media could show up there."

I stared at her. Trevor had turned on the back-porch light. He had moved back from Emmie and was standing several feet away – far enough not to crowd me, but close enough to hear everything that was taking place. With his hands in his pockets, he leaned against the bannister. He was still dressed in the clothes he'd worn to the funeral, but he'd ditched his tie and coat.

"And where do you suggest I go? I know that Butch is a regular visitor to your house. I'm not intruding into your life."

She glanced away.

"And I'd rather not go to my parents' house, Emmie, for several reasons."

"I have four empty bedrooms," Trevor chimed in.

I glanced at him. I felt like I'd been ignoring him.

"Five, if you count the fully furnished apartment below us. My parents used to rent it out to medical college students."

"Trevor, I couldn't."

"Grace, several people could live in this house and never run into each other for days. Trust me, I know. So, I can give you all the space you need, and you'll be safe here. And I promise to be a perfect gentleman."

"Trevor's right, Grace. You should stay here," Emmie interjected.

"Really? I didn't think you approved."

She furrowed her brow and looked puzzled.

"Grace, I know that it wasn't you who ended your marriage."

I stared at her, giving her that "shut up" look she knew well. Her eyes widened.

"You didn't tell Trevor yet?"

"I did, but who told you?"

She took a deep breath.

"Please, like I didn't know. Besides, Drew's been staying at Zack's house some and Butch's, which is the reason Butch has been staying at my house a lot."

I raised an eyebrow at her.

"Okay, one of the reasons. But my days with Butch are numbered. He's been different over the past couple of weeks, and Drew has gotten worse. Since Drew left you, he's been angry all the time – no filter. Drew got the letter yesterday saying your divorce was final. Butch saw it on his coffee table when he stopped by the house, but he didn't see Drew. We think he went on a bender, and then this woman winds up dead today."

"Do you think he was seeing her? I've been worried about him for the past week. I just knew something terrible was about to happen."

"Did you have another dream?"

"Several. Can I see Drew?"

"Butch said you might ask, but I don't think you can right now. He's just been arrested. He has to go before a judge, and Butch said there's a huge chance he won't get bail especially if he's charged with murder. At the very least, he could be charged with voluntary manslaughter. If bond is set, it could be very high. There might not be any way he will get out."

I didn't know what to say. I didn't want to have to make any type of decision. I really wanted someone to make it for me.

"He didn't do whatever they've accused him of, Emmie. I know it. You can't convince me otherwise."

19

An awkward silence fell as I stared at Emmie. I'd thought about my strange final conversation with Drew a lot and now maybe it made a little more sense. Maybe this was what he was asking my help for, but where would I even start?

Trevor had said very little to this point, but he took the pause as an opportunity to intervene.

"Emmie, why don't you call Beth and see if she can handle things for Grace for the rest of the week? That would give you peace of mind, wouldn't it, Grace?"

I gave a weak "yes."

"She can stay here with me; unless there's somewhere else you'd rather go?" he looked at me. I didn't know how to answer. I couldn't spend the night here, could I?

"I don't want to go anywhere, but I don't have any other clothes. I need to go home."

"Well, sweetie, we've already determined you can't go home yet," Emmie said.

"Emmie, would you do Grace a favor? Get her something to wear for a couple of days," he reached into his pocket and pulled out some bills. I have no idea how much money he gave Emmie. "Would you go get her anything she needs so she doesn't have to worry? A toothbrush, toiletries, everything. Please."

"Trevor, you don't have to do that," I objected.

"Grace, consider it a Christmas gift. Consider it a friend helping out a friend. Don't worry about it."

Emmie glanced back and forth between Trevor and me. I thought about arguing, but I was spent. The divorce, his mother's death, and now this.

"I'll stay here," I said weakly.

"Besides, I know what you're thinking, Grace," Emmie said. "If you're here, you can start trying to figure out what's really going on with Drew."

I managed a weak smile.

"Whatever she needs," he said. "You know her."

"It's Christmastime so this could take a while."

He looked at me and back at her.

"I know this is an imposition," he said.

"No, Grace is my best friend and is never an imposition. I'm just telling you it could take a while."

"We're not going anywhere, and I promise I'll take care of her," he said, and I was pretty sure he winked at her.

He walked Emmie to the front door. I wondered what they were talking about. I assumed it would have to be me. I couldn't believe Drew would kill someone. I mean, it was always a possibility in the line of duty that he might have to fire at a suspect, but he wouldn't murder someone. He believed in upholding the law, not breaking it. Despite the anger and grief I'd seen in him, I never believed he could physically harm me or anyone else.

I stared off into the night. Drew could spend his life behind bars, not the best place for a police officer. I couldn't imagine what he was going through. My heart ached for him. I couldn't help that I still loved him. I kept repeating that last conversation in my head. How was I going to help him? I wanted to hate him, but I couldn't. I knew that his grief and addiction were tearing him apart. I was torn too, but I also knew that I was going to have to find a way to help Drew. That wasn't going to make anyone happy. The dream I'd had a few days before was hazy, but in it, I knew that Drew was in trouble, and this time, I was the one who helped him. It didn't change our relationship, but it saved him from the situation he was in. The dream didn't spell out that he'd been arrested in a suspicious death. It just told me he was in trouble and needed me. It gave me a sense of peace that everything would work out, but I knew this was going to be painful because he didn't want me in his life. I wasn't sure how long it was before Trevor returned. I was still sitting with my arms wrapped around my knees and lost in thought when he sat down next to me.

"Grace, do you want to come inside?" he asked gently as he sat down next to me.

I glanced at him.

"I'm okay."

"I've got a pair of sweats and a T-shirt you could change into. If you're going to sit like a pretzel, you should do it in more comfortable clothing."

I laughed. Despite all the sorrow over the past few weeks, there had been a lot of laughter. I guess I did need to get out of this dress.

"I'll pay you back whatever you gave Emmie."

"You don't need to worry about any of that right now."

"You don't have to do any of this."

He touched my hand and locked his eyes with mine.

"When I first came back to town, I told you I needed and wanted a friend, and that I knew that's all you were able to give. You have been an incredible friend to me. More of a friend than I could've ever asked for. You've been so much more though. I've relied on you and you've been more of an emotional support than you realize. I want to be here for you," he said. "I haven't been there for you like you needed me."

"Don't be ridiculous, Trevor. Your mother needed you, and I wouldn't have traded these last few weeks for anything. Watching you with her was the most amazing thing. Helping you, being that support for you, seeing you with Miss Harper is probably the only thing that has gotten me through these past few weeks. It shook me out of my pity parties, and I needed that. Every time the thought that I was dying inside came to me, I realized how stupid that sounded. I wasn't dying inside. Yes, I've hurt like I never had in my life, but I was still very much alive." I paused. "I don't want to love Drew. I don't want my heart to hurt."

"I know, Grace. I know."

"I see things in the tabloids at the grocery store checkout about stars getting divorced and remarried or living with someone at the drop of the hat. I don't understand. I'm not made like that."

"You gave him 14 years of your life. I understand. You didn't expect that he'd leave. In your mind, you never thought he'd divorce you. While things weren't great with him, you said you'd always love him and stick by him. That's who you are so all of this will take time for you to adjust."

"I believed in 'til death us do part.'"

"I know. I'm glad you feel that way."

I looked at him.

"Thank you."

He furrowed his brow.

"For what?"

"Being here, Trevor. Caring about me."

"I hear a 'but' in your voice. What's the matter?"

"You know that expression about if something's too good to be true, it probably is."

He looked confused.

"I think of that every time I see you," I said.

He chuckled.

"I'm not perfect, and if you stay with me a couple of days, you will learn that pretty fast. You've forgotten a lot about me in the 16 or so years since you've known me. Come on, let's go pick out a room for you and find something for you to change into."

Most of my time in the Blake house had been on the main floor, although I had been in the downstairs apartment before. I'd never ventured above the mahogany staircase in the main part of the house though. I had no idea what the rest of the house even looked like. I'd imagined it, and I was sure it looked like the first floor.

"As I said, there are five empty bedrooms; there is a sixth bedroom, but it's mine. I'd prefer you didn't stay in my parents' room. But that still leaves four. There are two empty bedrooms not including my parents' room, on the second floor near my room; one in the basement, and one in the attic. I won't tell you which one to pick, but I have an idea of which one you might like. I'll have to get some sheets because I honestly have no idea how long it's been since any of these rooms have been occupied. They could be musty and dusty."

I followed him up the staircase.

At the top of the landing, he turned.

"My room is on this end of the hallway, and the room I'm talking about is on the other end. When my father became ill and bedridden, we moved him downstairs into the same room my mother stayed in at the end of her life. She closed their room and moved into the bedroom I'm going to take you to. It belonged to my brother, James, originally. My mother wanted a feminine room, so she remodeled it. It's not modern by any stretch of the imagination though."

We walked to the end of the hallway, and he opened the door. It took my breath away. It felt Victorian. There was no other way to describe it. The focal point was the antique four poster, canopy bed accented with swaths of gauzy white fabric. The bedding was white and was accented with numerous pillows in shades of pink. Some had hot pink stripes; others had a rose motif. The hardwoods had several accent rugs in keeping with the theme of the room. The massive windows were only covered with sheer curtains and Venetian blinds. I walked over to the cherry-wood dresser. It was dotted with lace doilies. A beautiful silver hairbrush engraved with Miss Harper's initial lay in the center of it. There were two hurricane lamps on either side of the massive mirror.

A set of French doors dressed with the same gauzy curtains, allowing the moonlight to cascade in, led out to the back porch. In the corner of the room was a window seat with velvet cushions. He was right. I'd fallen in love with the room. Now, if I only had a few books.

"What do you think?"

"I think I could move in here and never leave."

The words tumbled out of my mouth without thought. I realized I'd uttered them out loud only when he began to laugh. I turned away in embarrassment. I couldn't believe I'd just said that to him.

"I'm glad you like it. My mother had a romantic side, and you have one too. That's the reason I showed you this one first. But it's set a few decades ago."

I laughed.

"A little more than a few decades ago; more like a century ago. Romance never goes out of style though. I sometimes think I was born in the wrong era."

I glanced back at him. He walked to the French doors and opened them.

"This leads to the porch on the back of the house and connects the rooms on this side of the house. My room is on the far end."

I followed him onto the porch which had a swing and a few chairs. It was similar to the porch we'd left directly below. The rain had stopped again.

"It's beautiful out tonight even with the rain," I said.

He walked up next to me. I glanced at him as he stared out into the distance. I was concerned about him. It had been hard for him since he returned to Augusta.

"Enough about me, Trevor. How are you doing? It's been a rough couple of months for you. And you've held it together too well the past few days."

He didn't answer right away.

"I'd rather focus on you. Focusing on others helps me take my mind off things," he said before turning toward me. "We knew this was going to happen. I know she's not in pain any longer, and I'm so grateful I came back here to spend these last few months with her. We reconnected, and you brought her a lot of joy."

"I think that her son was the one who brought her the joy," I said as I put my hand on his arm. "You always told me you were her favorite."

He took a deep breath and smiled.

"Well, I like to think that I'm her favorite. Rather was her favorite," he paused. "I can't get used to saying 'was.' Even though we were expecting it, it's still hard. And I just realized how exhausted I am."

"You should be. The days and nights have been long. I can't imagine you've slept much because you were by her side most of the time. You don't need to babysit me. I can let Emmie in when she gets back."

"It will be nice to sleep in my own bed again. I've slept downstairs on the couch next to her for most of the past several weeks."

"Like I said, you don't have to worry about me."

He didn't reply. He just nodded in affirmation.

"Follow me, and I'll get you something to change into."

We walked back down the hallway.

"There's a bathroom in between our rooms in case you want to shower."

"Thank you, Trevor."

I walked into his room. I'd never been in it before. It was a masculine room, but there were still hints that it hadn't been altered since he was a teenager. The room looked more like a study with a bed in the middle of it. It had several built-in bookcases, and they were full of books. There were many classic titles there – Huckleberry Finn, Tom Sawyer, Robinson Crusoe. He'd always loved to read. Under the bookcases was a desk. Everything was neat and in order. I was surprised to see our prom picture on his desk. There were a couple of posters on the wall – mainly of sportscars.

He pulled out of pair of sweatpants and a T-shirt and handed them to me. They were neatly folded; they looked like they could've been ironed. Trevor was fastidious. I imagined he was a neat freak. He smiled.

"Yes, those have been ironed, and yes, I know how to do it myself. I've been on my own for a while. I'm a little set in my ways."

I smiled back.

"I told you I wasn't perfect. I like things in order, maybe too much order," he said.

I looked at those beautiful tousled blonde curls of his and

smiled.

"What?"

I glanced away and laughed.

"Nothing, but some things we can't control, now can we?"

"The hair?" he asked and started to laugh. "After all these years, I've finally gotten used to the curls. I tried slicking them back or cutting them, but Mama always loved my curls. I grew them back out for her."

"I always liked them too."

He tilted his head and smiled.

"Oh really?"

I glanced away; I was embarrassed again.

"Thanks for the clothes. I'm going to take a shower."

I needed a shower. The warm water beating on my back and shoulders felt so good. I wanted to use every last drop of hot water. I didn't tell Trevor the real reason I didn't want to go to sleep. I hadn't had a dream in six weeks. Well, not a full-blown, cinematic dream like I usually had. There were gray shadows at night, and I woke up just knowing that Drew was in danger. There were no details. Now I had this feeling that if I went to sleep, I'd have one, and I wasn't sure what it might tell me.

After my shower, I made my way back to the porch. The air was still, and the temperature somewhere in the 60s. It was a gorgeous night. I sat on the swing, which creaked as I began to move on it.

I wondered who Drew had called when he was arrested. I'd assumed it was his mother. She was definitely one person who blamed me for our divorce. She resented me for not having her grandchildren. That was another failure I didn't bring up earlier. I fidgeted with the rings on my hand. I felt stripped without them. They were one constant in my life.

"I thought you were tired," I heard a voice behind me. I turned to see Trevor.

"No, I'm wide awake, besides someone has to let Emmie back

in. You were the one who was exhausted, or so I thought. You should rest, Trevor. These past few months have taken a toll."

"Have you ever been so tired you couldn't sleep?"

"Yeah, I think I'm there now."

"Care to talk about it?"

"No."

He laughed.

"Okay. Let me put it another way. Will you talk with me about what's bothering you, Grace, please?"

I was reluctant to say anything. I didn't share my dreams with too many people, even the ones who knew I had them.

"I – "

"You can tell me anything," he said softly. "I'll always listen to you."

Despite his statement, I hesitated.

"You know those dreams I used to have – the ones at night that were -"

"Prophetic?" he finished my sentence.

"I guess that's a good word for them, but yes those."

"I do."

"Well, it's been a while, but I have this feeling that -"

"That you're going to have one tonight."

"Yeah."

"Why do you think that, Grace?"

"I can't explain it."

"Do you usually know?"

"Sometimes, I do. Sometimes, I've breathed a sigh of relief that I haven't had one in a while, and bam, there's one."

"Are you sure you just aren't worked up with the divorce and Drew's arrest?"

"Do you think I make all this up?"

I bristled.

"No, that's not what I meant."

"A lot of times the things I see in them I never could've

known outside of the context of the dream. I shouldn't have said anything to you. I try to keep that quiet because people like you think I'm crazy."

"Whoa – people like me? Grace, I never said you were crazy or that your dreams made you different."

"That's how it sounded."

"I'm a man of science, but I also have faith. You should know that. Mama raised me to believe things I still believe. You can't take it away. There are things I've seen that I can't explain. Things that have made no logical sense. I've had several patients whose prognosis was grim, but they had strong faith and made it through despite the odds. Many of them said it was strong faith and prayer, combined with their medical treatment. I've seen others who should've pulled through, but they didn't make it. There's no rhyme or reason to cancer."

I bit my lip and looked away. If he didn't believe in me, I wasn't going through that again. At least at the very end of our relationship, Drew told me to trust my dreams and my instinct. They'd never lead me astray. At least I had that. It helped some, but it didn't make up for the rest of the pain.

Trevor reached out to touch my hand to get me to look at him. I could see his face in the moonlight. He was tender as he spoke to me, and unlike when Drew talked to me, Trevor didn't make me feel like a child.

"Grace, I do believe you about the dreams. When I left for Georgia, my mother turned my room into a shrine. I told you I was her favorite of all her sons. I think she knew about my dad's affair with Bill's mom. I was born after Bill, and she often told me I was her 'kiss from Heaven.' I gave her a lot of comfort. She remodeled all my brothers' rooms, but she didn't touch mine. My room is basically a time capsule from 15 years ago. It hasn't been changed since I dated you."

"I noticed that."

I wasn't sure why he was telling me this.

"Sure, I came home for brief periods of time, but I didn't go in the closets or drawers. A couple of weeks ago, I started doing some cleaning, and I found a box of things you'd given to me including the cards."

I smiled. I loved greeting cards, and I bought them for him randomly. God only knows what I wrote in them. I have always been a romantic at heart, and I was much worse when I was a teenager before the painful reality of adulthood had struck.

"In some of them, you wrote about some of the dreams you had."

I vaguely remembered writing them down and giving them to him. I wish I knew what was on those cards now.

"In one of them, you saw my older brothers and me in front of a football stadium where everyone was wearing red and black except us. The four of us were wearing white coats. My three brothers were smiling, but you wrote that I looked sad and angry. That was my senior year of high school - before my father started insisting I go to Georgia. I'd already been accepted at Augusta State."

I took a deep breath as he continued.

"White coats are doctors. You saw the stadium, red and black. That would be the University of Georgia. They are all happy doctors, but I was not. And as I said, that was during my rebellious phase when I thought I was actually going to get to do what I wanted with my life, not what my father wanted."

"Is that the only one?"

He winked at me.

"That's the only one I want to share with you - now. The point is you were right even though I hated you were."

Right off, I couldn't think of any other dreams I'd had that I'd actually shared with him. I wasn't sure if I'd dreamed of marrying him or just fantasized about it. And if I had would I have even told him?

"I'm just afraid of what might be in my dreams. I've seen some horrible things in them – human trafficking, people dying."

"You said you'd dreamed about Drew."

"Nothing definite. Gray, hazy shadows. I just knew he was in danger. Usually, those prophetic dreams or whatever you want to call them are in technicolor and big screen."

He laughed.

"I want to help him."

I told him about the conversation Drew and I had at my car after we'd signed the divorce papers.

"Trevor, after what he said. I think this is a set-up. I don't know why, but I know him. He wouldn't murder someone. I could see self-defense. I could see as a last resort, but not cold-blooded gunning someone down. I'm just curious about this woman."

"I understand that you still love him. Fourteen years is a long time, and you truly believe and live out what you were taught in Sunday school about love. It hopes all, believes all, endures all, and it never fails."

"I'm sorry. I don't want to - "

He put his finger on my lips and shook his head. He leaned in close and spoke gently.

"You don't have to apologize. I get it, but the two of you aren't married anymore. It was his choice, and he hasn't contacted you in almost two months, has he?"

I broke his gaze and glanced down at my hands.

"No, he hasn't, and I stopped trying to contact him."

Trevor sighed and put his hand over mine. I glanced up at him.

"If you want to help him, I'll lend whatever resources I can to help you."

I didn't understand why he'd want to help.

"Maybe this will give you closure or peace or whatever it is you're looking for," he said.

He had an uncanny way of reading my mind. He got up.

"What's wrong?" I asked.

"The doorbell. I guess I'm used to it. I can hear it out here."

"I didn't hear it."

"I know."

"You go to sleep. I'll see about Emmie. Goodnight, Trevor."

I walked downstairs to find Emmie with a mountain of bags.

"He said a couple of days. What have you done, Emmie?"

"I had money and a great excuse to shop. What else did I need?"

"Just exactly how much money do I owe him?"

She smiled at me.

"I'm not telling you that, but Jimmy Hughes will need to have a lot of fights with Peggy."

"Great. That much?"

Emmie laughed, and I sighed.

"You have to see this room," I said as I took some of the bags from her, leading her up the staircase.

"Wow, this is definitely you," Emmie said as she stepped into the room. "I love this bed. It's so romantic."

She turned around at winked at me.

"So you're a free woman now, and there's one incredibly handsome man in the other room."

"Stop. You know that's not me. I still hurt, and what if I screw another relationship up? I mean, Trevor was the first man to break my heart."

"Sweetie, he was only like 19."

"It didn't make it hurt any less and that was the first time you and I binged on ice cream. I've never been so sick in my life, and we did it several weekends in a row. I didn't learn my lesson obviously. And it took me more than a year before I wanted to even think about dating anyone. I gave Drew almost 14 years of my life, more if you consider when I was a kid and daydreamed about him. I need time."

"I know, sweetie. You are going to need to go and talk to them at the sheriff's department. Butch said he'd go with you."

"That would be a good idea. I'll be ready first thing in the morning."

"I'm going home. Beth and I have everything covered for

the next couple of days. I know how close you and Miss Harper got before she died. You need to take time for you. I put a couple of the latest bestsellers in there too. If you aren't going to occupy your time with Trevor, go read. I'd pick Trevor over books though."

I smiled.

"Thanks for the advice, Emmie, but I have a case to solve first."

"I can only do so much," Emmie said and let out a long sigh.

I followed her back downstairs and locked the door behind her.

When I'd taken my shower earlier, I noticed a small blanket in the linen closet. I'd brought it into the room. I decided to plug my phone in. I hadn't looked at in hours; I was sure the battery was low if I had any left at all. I kept my charger in my purse at all times because the phone never seemed to hold a charged battery all day. I looked at it. Before I powered it off, I noticed a voicemail. The only missed calls I'd had were from Emmie. I figured it must've been from her, but I decided to listen to it anyway.

"Hey, Gracie, babe," I almost dropped the phone. It was Drew. Was I his one phone call, and I missed it? I didn't catch the time and date. Maybe he called before the arrest. I was in a daze. Immediately tears started flowing. "Listen I only have a second. Do you remember what I told you after we'd met with the judge about our divorce? I meant it."

He tried to sound harsh, but there was something about his voice. It sounded fearful instead. I knew the nuances in his voice. He'd never sounded that way before. There was something about the tone. It wasn't the "my case, Grace. My case" angry tone I knew so well. It wasn't the tone that had accused me of having an affair with Trevor or accused Trevor of murder. I wasn't sure what was different, but I knew I had to pay attention to every inflection and every single word.

"Tell Zack he has one mean right hook. And don't forget to pay the mortgage payment this month, okay? And I really meant everything I said that day."

And he hung up.

The one phone call he gets, and I blow it. I wondered what he meant because that message wasn't straightforward. I felt sick to my stomach. How did I miss the call? Well that was a stupid question, thinking back over the day.

I didn't get in the bed, but I wrapped myself in the blanket and curled up in the window seat. I stared out the window and watched as water droplets coursed from the top of the panes to the bottom. I fought sleep for as long as I could. I knew that if he called me, he was cashing in on that favor he'd asked of me. But how was I supposed to help him? I wasn't in law enforcement. If he didn't trust anyone, how was I supposed to know who I could trust.

Finally sleep won out, and right on cue, what I'd dreaded overtook me. I wasn't sure what I expected to dream.

I was in a warehouse that looked eerily like the one where the girls had been housed in April while the golf tournament was in town. It was that same warehouse, where I'd met Jazzy after Jillian, the leader of the group, had me kidnapped. I thought I was going to die that weekend.

I could hear voices.

"He should've known better than to mess with us," said a male voice I didn't recognize. "Why don't we just kill him?"

"Kill him. He needs to suffer for what he's done. Killing him will be too easy. We'll start with ruining his career, and then we'll make everyone important to him suffer," another voice said.

The voices were muffled, and there was an echo. Men? Women? In the dream, I couldn't tell. What had he done that was so horrible? Why would they do this?

"This all has to look like Drew did it. Everything about the crime scene has to look like he killed her. Drag him over here."

I had a sinking feeling. There was an echo. One of the voices sounded vaguely familiar, but I couldn't place it right off. It was distorted.

Whoever was talking had a flashlight. He shone it on the ground, but there was already some light in the room. It wasn't completely dark. I think the light was coming in from above. Maybe there were windows in the warehouse. I wasn't sure. I walked closer in the dream. I watched as one of the men positioned Drew's body. I couldn't see the man's face. I wondered if he was a deputy. Then, everything went black for a minute. I heard a woman's voice. She was crying and begging for her life; then there was a scream followed by two gunshots. I'm glad I didn't witness the murder; hearing her cries for help were hard enough.

"We need to place him perfectly for the angle of the shot. Put the gun in his hand."

I saw two figures throw Drew onto the floor. He was unconscious. They placed the gun in his hand. The woman's body was nearby. She was covered in blood. Thankfully, I couldn't see her face. She was turned away from me. It was as though I was standing in the middle of everything. I turned to see who was behind me. There was a deputy. I took a deep breath. I didn't recognize him.

"No one can help you now, Investigator Drew Ward. They will put you behind bars forever."

"Put the gun in his hand. Splash some alcohol on his clothes. It will look like he's been here for a few hours; by then, his blood alcohol level will have dropped. Tests won't show he's that drunk, but the drugs in his system should keep him out for a while. We can time it so someone comes before they completely wear off."

"Are you sure those drugs won't show up? Everybody knows Drew doesn't use. He might drink, but he doesn't touch drugs."

"We'll have our guy put in a call to 911 soon enough."

I heard laughter. It was chilling. I felt cold and scared. The warehouse wasn't completely dark. The doors were open, and light streamed in. Why didn't they do this in the dark? Drew was out for a while. I stood there and watched. Of course, time means nothing in a dream.

"We'll plant some evidence in his car. His DNA is on her,

and his prints are on the gun. We have some witnesses who'll say they were arguing at a club It will be open and shut. He'll appear to have been drunk. He won't remember what happened. He'll get life at least."

They left, and Drew slept. His face was bruised. I could see that. Drew started to sit up. He was dazed as he looked around. He saw the body and was bent over her when two deputies arrived and arrested him. It was so scripted. He dropped the gun and threw his hands in the air. I watched as they put his hands behind him and clamped handcuffs on him. I watched as they read him his rights.

Whenever I had a dream, it was like someone grabbed me by my shoulders and shook me to wake me up. Remembering the details was vital. I was still partially asleep as I stood up, planning to grab the notebook where I'd written down dozens of them. Then I realized I wasn't at home, and I had nothing to write with or on. I had no idea where Trevor kept a pen and paper. It was something about the physical act of writing it. Typing it on my phone didn't have the same effect. When I wrote it, it hardwired it back to my brain or something. I couldn't explain it.

I rushed down the hall to Trevor's room. I hesitated at the door and went downstairs instead.

Maybe there was something in the kitchen. I didn't even know where to begin to look, so I just started opening drawers.

"You won't find a midnight snack there."

I jumped at the sound of Trevor's voice.

"I'm sorry. I was trying to be quiet, Trevor. I didn't mean to wake you."

"I'm a light sleeper. What are you doing?"

"I need some paper and a pen."

He raised an eyebrow.

"I promise if you'll get me some paper and a pen I'll tell you everything. Just let me write it down first."

I didn't have time to think about what the dream meant or any of that. I just needed to write it down, and I'd figure it out later.

He went to one drawer I hadn't looked in yet and pulled out a pen and paper and handed it to me. I sat down at the table and tried to write out every detail. Before I could finish, Trevor had sat down across from me. He'd sliced a couple of pieces of chocolate cake, leftover from the funeral, and a glass of milk. There was one for me and one for him.

As soon as I finished, I looked up to see him staring at me.

"Thanks."

"Emmie said chocolate is the way to your heart."

"Did she now?"

He smiled and winked at me.

"This cake is pretty good. You should try it, Grace."

"I didn't mean to wake you."

"It wouldn't have taken much to wake me. I was worried about you anyway. I don't really think I was asleep. When I slept on the couch next to Mama's hospital bed, I stirred every time she did. She'd be in pain in the middle of the night sometimes, so I was there if she needed anything. I can't get used to the idea she's not here. I'm glad you're here. "

"You should get some rest."

"I will, but I'm curious as to why you are up at 3:30 in the morning."

I'd taken a bite of the cake, and it practically melted in my mouth; it was so good.

"I was his phone call."

Trevor tilted his head.

"What?"

"Drew's phone call from jail. Or at least I think it was from jail. I had a voicemail on my phone with no missed call. I don't know how I missed it."

I thought I might start crying again. He needed me, and I wasn't there.

"What did he say?"

"It was cryptic. My phone is upstairs. I'll listen again when

I'm more awake. And then I had a dream - " I paused. I reached out for Trevor's hand, looked into his eyes and held his gaze. "Drew didn't do whatever he's accused of. I have to help him – somehow."

I slid the paper across the table to him.

"If you can make out my chicken scratch, you're welcome to read it."

He picked up the notebook.

"I write them down, so I don't forget, and then I see how accurate they are. I wish they weren't sometimes."

He read through it and looked at me.

"I think we have some long days ahead of us," he said as he returned it to me.

"Thank you for believing in me. This cake is too rich. I can't believe I ate all of that."

"Do you think you can sleep now?"

"I don't know. I'll have a sugar rush."

"Good night, Grace," he said. "Try to get some sleep."

He stood up and kissed me on the top of my head.

I tried to take that advice, but my adrenaline was pumping. Or maybe it was the sugar I'd just eaten. What was I thinking?

I pulled out my phone to find out more about this woman he supposedly killed.

I found several social media profiles with the name of Vanessa Graham, but none of them were linked to Augusta. It probably wasn't a good idea, but I decided to read some of the articles about Drew. I cried reading the narratives. They were simple, cut and dry. Nothing that told me what really took place; of course, they couldn't know that. Did Drew even know what really happened? In this case, I trusted my dream. I believed he'd been drugged; I believed he didn't know. The woman's name wasn't mentioned. It just said it would be released upon the notification of next of kin so there were no photos of her either. The official statement from the department was that it was under investigation, and he was being held. It didn't say anything about charges. I guess it was still too early for that.

By 6 a.m., I decided to get dressed. It was too late to

try to go back to sleep. All I could do was pray that this turned out all right. I'd have to wear the funeral dress again. I didn't have anything else appropriate to wear. Fortunately, Emmie brought toiletries and a little makeup. She thought of everything. If they said anything else about me in the news media, I wanted it to be that his wife was cooperating with the investigation.

I tiptoed down the hall. I'd hoped Trevor had gotten some sleep at least. I could make breakfast before getting dressed. I used to enjoy breakfast because of the good times I had making it with Drew. But since he'd left, I hadn't made breakfast. If I ate anything, it was something quick and easy – a banana or a doughnut or something like that.

I sent Beth a text to thank her for keeping watch over the shop.

Jazzy and I are having a great time. We're remodeling.

Great. I had no idea what that meant, but I had too much on my mind to try and figure that out.

I had no idea what was in Trevor's refrigerator besides macaroni and cheese, casseroles, and several pies. I definitely didn't want any of that for breakfast, but he didn't seem to have any fresh vegetables. I knew he hadn't been to the grocery store in several days. The last week of his mother's life he barely left her bedside. She'd been in the hospital, but she requested to be taken off all treatment. She wanted to die at home surrounded by family and friends. She had plenty of medical expertise at her fingertips. During her last few weeks, Trevor ate a lot of takeout. He didn't cook much at all. And I wasn't a gourmet chef by any stretch of the imagination.

It wasn't going to be filled with healthy choices. Instead, it would be filled with Southern options. There was plenty of fried chicken and some biscuits and I think there was even gravy. I hadn't had a breakfast like this since my grandmother was alive.

I found a tray and tried to make a great presentation of the open-faced biscuits with chicken and gravy. I found one of the arrangements I'd made for Miss Harper and took a few of the carnations and lilies that were still in good shape, added some greenery, and put them in a vase. It looked pretty. I had never worked as a waitress, so I wasn't great at carrying trays. I took a deep breath before I headed up the stairs.

Trevor's door was slightly open, and I used my hip to push it the rest of the way.

"Good morning, sunshine."

He stirred slowly and looked up at me.

"It's still dark, Grace. What time is it?"

"6:30. You can go back to sleep when I leave."

I waited for him to sit up and then I gave him the tray. I sat down on the bed.

"And to what do I owe this?"

"You've been taking care of your mother 24/7 for four months. When was the last time anyone did anything for you?"

"Grace, you've done more for me since coming back into my life than you realize. Just having someone to talk to and care has taken a burden off me."

"Okay, well now I'm feeding you. Granted, Dr. Blake, it's not exactly the best food for you. You need to go grocery shopping, by the way."

"Cooking and you tried to clean my kitchen last night. You are still my guest, Grace."

"Well if I stay here much longer, I'll probably do laundry and maybe mop those floors. Who knows I may even give your walls a fresh coat of paint, and I'd really love to get my hands in your soil."

"What?"

"Your mother's gardens. I'd love to tend them."

"Nervous?"

"Very."

"Are you still going to try to see him?

I took a deep breath.

"I feel like I have to especially after he left that cryptic message on my phone. I'm sorry."

"Why are you sorry? You do what you have to do. I can see you're on a mission."

"Thank you."

3

I changed my mind at the last minute and decided I didn't want Butch to take me to the station. Trevor insisted on taking me. He didn't want me to be alone at least on the ride there and back.

Butch met me outside the sheriff's offices to escort me to Capt. Howard.

"Butch, does anyone else know that the divorce is final besides you, Emmie, and Trevor?"

"I haven't told anyone, and Drew hasn't said a word about it, even to me. People have only been making assumptions. Unless someone was paying attention to the divorce records they probably don't know."

"Butch, I have to see him. It's vital."

"Grace, you're not going to be able to. Emmie and Drew have told me about the dreams you have. Did you have another one?"

"Yes. I've had a couple, but nothing definite. They've been hazy."

I didn't tell him the complete truth and I stopped myself from saying something about my phone call from Drew. I kept hearing Drew's voice in my head telling me he didn't know who to trust. I figured it might be best for me not to say anything. It had become also instinctive to play my dreams off to someone I didn't know that well. That's the reason I didn't give him details. Butch seemed agitated.

"Butch, do you think someone could've set Drew up?"

"Someone as in? What are you getting at?"

He narrowed his eyes at me. It frightened me.

"Nothing."

He waited for me to say something else, but when I didn't, he started moving toward the door for me to follow.

"I'm taking you to Capt. Will Howard. He's over homicide, so he's over Drew."

"I think I met him once or twice."

Things started blurring around me. I just followed Butch as he walked me through. I felt like a robot. I was trying to gather my thoughts. Butch had given me an idea of what types of questions I might be asked. I was focused. I needed to see Drew.

I had met Capt. Howard a couple of times. He was always professional and courteous to me. When Drew was promoted in the spring, his mother had a small party, and Drew invited Capt. Howard and his wife. That party was a blur though. At the time, I was still having problems getting past that first murder investigation I found myself a part of. I didn't sleep much for several weeks. I didn't know what to expect out of this meeting. Everyone knew that Drew and I had separated at least. I was concerned with that. I didn't know who knew he and I were divorced. And I wondered about Drew's warning that he didn't know who he could trust.

"Mrs. Ward, thank you for coming in," Capt. Howard looked up as I came in. He stood and shook my hand. Then he motioned for me to take a seat.

I didn't say anything. I obediently sat down. I grasped my hands together in my lap because I knew they were trembling. I knew I had to be careful with my words, but I wasn't sure what I could do about my expressions. They tended to get me into trouble because my face didn't lie. I wanted to trust him, but could I?

"I need to ask you some questions. You know your husband has been arrested in the suspicious death of a woman."

"Yes, sir. I do."

"When was the last time you saw your husband?"

"Oct. 27," I said.

"He hasn't been living with you."

"No."

I figured it was best to say as little as possible and to answer without expounding.

"When did he move out?"

"He left on Oct. 15."

"Do you know where he's been living?"

"Butch – I mean Deputy Childress told me that Drew had been staying with him some, and he's stayed with my brother, First Sgt. Zack Burke."

"Did Drew have a substance abuse problem?"

Substance abuse. I swallowed.

"Can you clarify that?"

He looked at me. He seemed aggravated.

"Did he take drugs?"

"No. He never even took aspirin for a headache."

Too much information; too many words. Just stick to the facts. I told myself.

"Did he have a drinking problem?"

I hesitated. I didn't want to incriminate him, but I didn't want to lie.

"What do you mean?"

He narrowed his eyes at me. He didn't seem happy.

"Let me rephrase that. Did he drink?"

"Yes."

"Do you think his drinking was a problem?"

I had to think fast. I knew this was coming. I'd played it over and over in my brain, hoping my face wouldn't give away my real feelings on the subject.

"Sir, I'm not sure what you mean by a 'problem.' I personally don't drink so I believe most drinking is a problem."

He stared at me and blinked several times. He didn't have a smile. He simply stared and then he started writing again. Oh God, please let my face have been expressionless. Somehow, though, I don't think that was a prayer that was answered the way I wanted.

"Was your husband having an affair when you separated?"

That stung. Drew having an affair. I think that must've gotten a reaction because he started writing something down.

"I always believed he was faithful."

"Do you know a woman by the name of Vanessa Graham?"

"No, sir, I do not. All I know is that is the name of the woman Drew is accused of killing."

He glanced at me when I said that and raised an eyebrow.

"Did your husband keep secrets from you?"

"I'm sure that most married couples have things they don't tell each other."

"Mrs. Ward, did you study to be a lawyer?"

Was I supposed to laugh at that? It sounded like a joke, but I knew I had to be very careful with my words. Anything I said would be evidence against Drew.

"No, sir. I have a degree in business, and I own a business. I'm just trying to answer your questions as succinctly as possible. Do you have any more?"

"Not right now."

"Could I see my husband?"

I blurted that out. I wasn't sure how much longer I'd be sitting in this office, so I took my chance. He stared at me and seemed to be summing up my request. I thought the answer might be "no," but he stood for a moment.

"You haven't seen him in nearly two months. Why do you want to see him now?"

"He called me, and I still love him. I just want to make sure he's okay."

He raised an eyebrow when I said Drew called me. Should I have said that? And that came out more desperate-sounding than I wanted. He didn't answer.

"What happened to him?" I asked.

He pursed his lips and shook his head at me.

"Sorry, Mrs. Ward, but I can't tell you that."

That sounded like Drew. I knew the answer, but I couldn't stop myself from asking. I wasn't sure I could hold this together much longer.

"He didn't do it. I know Drew. He didn't."

Capt. Howard stared at me without responding. I stared at him, wondering if he was part of this set-up. I knew it had to be someone in the department. Was it him?

"Are you planning on going out of town over the holidays?"

"No, sir. My family is here. I'll be with them."

"I need to make sure I have your correct number in case I need to call you."

"Can I see him?"

"No, ma'am, I'm sorry, but you can't."

I nodded. I figured as much. I just wanted him to know I'd gotten his phone call. I wanted him to know I cared.

I walked out of Capt. Howard's office to find Butch waiting for me.

"Are you okay?" Butch asked.

I took a deep breath and wiped the tears away. That seemed to be enough of an answer for him. He appeared concerned.

"No, but I'll eventually be okay when I get him out of jail."

Butch tilted his head and took a breath as though he was going to say something, but he stopped.

"I can walk myself out. I think."

"Let me escort you, Grace," he said. "Did you drive?"

"No, Trevor had a few things to do downtown, and he's going to come back and get me. I'll text him when we get outside."

It was a pretty day for December. The sun was out and the temperatures moderate. There was a light breeze.

"Pretty day," I offered as Butch hovered over me. I'd sent my text to Trevor, and he'd responded that he'd be back shortly.

"It is."

"You don't have to wait out here with me. I'm fine."

"No, Grace, I can tell you aren't fine."

He put his hands on his hips and looked at me. As he stared at me, I was aware of other people looking too. I saw a couple of deputies glaring at me. One of them was vaguely familiar, and he didn't seem happy. I wasn't sure why.

"You're right. I'm not fine. I want to crawl into a corner, curl into a little ball, and cry until there's nothing left to cry. And I really want to get out of here because people are staring."

Butch turned around.

"Yeah, don't worry about them."

"Who are they? They don't look happy."

"Everyone is shocked about Drew. They just can't believe it."

One of them started walking toward us. Butch didn't say anything else.

"Aren't you Drew's wife?" the deputy asked.

"Yes."

"I'm Patrick Steed. I think we met a couple of years ago," he held out his hand for me to shake it. I vaguely remembered him. "Listen, we're here for you. If you need anything."

I wasn't sure what to think. Again, Drew's words echoed in my mind about him not having anyone to trust. I tried to read his body language. Trevor had been teaching me a little about body language based on things I did.

"Thank you. Drew didn't do it," I blurted out.

"I believe you, ma'am," he said and handed me a piece of paper with his number on it.

"Then why do they?"

"If they believe he did it, it's because there's evidence to support it, Mrs. Ward. But know we're looking at every avenue," he said before turning away and acknowledging Butch.

"I'll stay here until Trevor arrives," Butch said.

I nodded. I wasn't good at small talk, and I was embarrassed about missing Drew's phone call, so I didn't say anything about it to Butch. He stood and waited for Trevor as though he was protecting me. It was comforting, but I just wanted to be alone. I wished I had driven myself this morning despite Trevor's protests. Butch glanced at his phone. He was making me nervous. I wasn't sure why he continued to stand next to me. I wished he'd just leave me, and I wasn't sure what to make of Deputy Steed. He seemed kind enough. Why did he give me his card?

"I'm sorry. I'm not really good at small talk, but you can go back to what you need to be doing. I'll be okay."

He shook his head.

"No ma'am."

"Please."

"Look, Grace. Drew made me promise him I'd keep you safe."

The thought of someone else keeping me safe for my hus-, would I ever stop calling him husband? I was sure I would eventually. The tears started flowing again. I thought back to the phone message. When Drew called me "Gracie," I knew that it meant he wanted to take care of me. Gracie was my name when I was a little girl, and I knew why he was doing that. My dad and my brother both called me "Gracie" when they were worried about me or when they wanted me to know they were there for me. And Drew had picked up that nickname too and used it at the same times. And he called me "babe." At times during our marriage, I'd wondered if my name was actually "Babe" and not "Grace." He always referred to me that way. I wondered if it was just habit that caused him to do it.

"I'm right outside the police station. I think I'm okay."

"Not until Trevor gets here."

I needed answers. I wondered just how much Butch knew.

"All right then, who was Vanessa Graham?"

Butch's jaw dropped, and I noticed his eye twitch.

"I don't know," he said, but I didn't believe him. He knew something he wasn't telling me.

"You lived with Drew. You should know something. Emmie said he was seeing her."

"It's possible. Drew didn't tell me everything he did, and I didn't ask," he said sharply.

"Do you believe he did this?"

As I asked that, Trevor pulled up. I wasn't getting anywhere anyway. There was no reaction on Butch's face and he simply said, "I'll talk to you soon, Grace."

I knew Trevor was full of questions. His concerned look said it all.   He had parked the car and gotten out to open my door.

"There's nothing to tell. They won't let me see him," I said as I got into the vehicle.

There was an uncomfortable pause. I wished there was a quicker way to get to his house. After several awkward moments of quiet, he broke the silence.

"We're having dinner guests so –"

It was odd that he said "we." He and I weren't a couple or at least I didn't think we were. And the last thing I wanted was to be around people.

"We are?"

"Emmie and Butch and possibly her boys."

"Okay."

"I could use some help in the kitchen if you're up to it."

"I'm not the best cook," I said blandly.

"Prep work is always time consuming. I could use a sous chef," he said and laughed. "I have lots of onions, peppers and other veggies that need cutting."

I laughed.

"Emmie's boys won't eat any of that."

"I have frozen chicken nuggets, and there's lots of macaroni and cheese leftover from yesterday."

"This is true. Are you sure you want dinner guests?"

"Absolutely. You need some company; besides I need some flowers for tonight. I was hoping you'd arrange them for me."

"Really?"

"Yes, I have a wholesale order coming to my house, just the elements. I need a creative eye to put them together."

"You have a whole room full of flowers, and you invited the creative eye to dinner."

Trevor didn't respond. I saw him clench his jaw and shake his head. I wondered what I'd said. He didn't say anything else the entire trip to his house. Once we arrived, I gathered a few of his bags and followed him into the kitchen. He put some of the items into the refrigerator. I looked over his shoulder to see what he had bought.

"What do you need me to do?" I asked.

He turned to look at me.

"Grace, why do you keep putting yourself down?"

"What are you talking about?"

He seemed surprised at that comment and gave me a gentle smile.

"You keep doing it, and you don't even realize it."

I shook my head. I wasn't sure what he was saying.

"In the car, you said that I invited the creative eye to dinner."

"Yes."

"No, the creative eye that I want to help me with the flowers is standing right in front of me."

"Emmie is the one."

"You keep talking like you're a failure, Grace. Listen, there's nothing wrong with being humble. No one wants to be around arrogant people, but you take it to the extreme. Self-deprecation and humility aren't the same thing. I know you don't want to come across as conceited, but you could never be that."

I looked down and took a breath. He was right. I was always taught to be humble and not prideful, but I wasn't sure how to be confident sometimes.

"You need to change the way you value things."

"What do you mean?"

"You have the wrong measuring stick when it comes to

success."

I didn't respond. I was trying to process what he was saying to me. His voice was firm, direct, but he was gentle and compassionate at the same time. He had a great doctor's bedside manner. Why did he want to leave that profession? I knew he had to be amazing at it.

"I don't know whose eyes you see yourself through but let me give you a glimpse into the way other people – the people who matter – see you. You are beautiful – inside and out. You have taken a young woman with no hope and no future and given her a job and a purpose. She was a homeless prostitute before you met her. With the help of your band of friends, led by you, you are giving Jazzy a better life, helping her get an education. I could stop there, but I won't."

He reached out for my hands and gripped them. His gaze forced me to look into his eyes.

"You are intelligent. Yes, Emmie is an artist. Yes, she's got more talent than most people, but you are the one who, in your mid-20s, started a floral shop. Most businesses close within a year of opening. Yours is still open, and you have a loyal customer base. And you're smart enough to hire people who are loyal and who have amazing skills. And you aren't too shabby when it comes to floral design either. I've seen what you can do. You brought such joy to my mother on her deathbed."

He paused as tears started to well up in his eyes.

I felt the tears stinging in my own eyes.

"Who does that, Grace? Who? She was dying, but she had such joy. She looked forward to those daily arrangements toward the end, and do you know why?"

His voice broke with his emotion. I saw the tears in his eyes as I stared at him.

"Because she loved you. She loved seeing you., Grace Those flowers were icing on the cake. It was you she wanted to see," he paused. "But those flowers brought genuine smiles, and the smiles they brought through her tremendous pain were worth those arrangements' weight in gold, Grace. You don't know what that did for me."

He paused again and glanced away. He dropped my hands as he wiped away the tears.

"I know she loved the flowers, but those last several days, she just wanted to see you. You were always kind, and you didn't want anything in return," he said and stopped. He gazed in to my eyes.

"Last and definitely not the least, you have an amazing family and friends who love you and would die for you."

That was true. I wiped away a few stray tears.

"So what if Drew Ward is too much of an idiot to see this? He threw it all away, and you shouldn't feel like a failure or a disgrace to your family or whatever it is you feel right now. And yet, you are determined to help him and clear his name. I don't understand how you could after what he's done to you. But he failed you, Grace. You didn't fail him, and his leaving you doesn't make you a failure "

He paused and turned his head away, so I couldn't see into his eyes. He started to say something then he shook his head.

"I've said enough."

I wondered what he wasn't saying. I fidgeted with my rings.

"I'm sorry," I said.

"There's nothing to be sorry for. You apologize for things that aren't even your fault. I think if a tornado ripped through Augusta and killed hundreds of people, you'd apologize for that too."

I laughed. It was strange to be crying one minute and laughing the next.

"What did he do to you, Grace? The Grace I knew was quiet, but she didn't put herself down. She didn't apologize for everything. She was full of life and joy. She wasn't afraid. I don't even remember her caring what people thought of her. She didn't care that people talked about her and her weird friends. I didn't think they were weird, but that's what they called Emmie and Beth."

"I know."

I glanced at my rings.

"If I could, I'd wipe all this pain away from you," he

whispered.

"I know, Trevor. I'm sorry. Can you just give me a few minutes?"

I needed to be alone. I needed to get away. I rushed up the stairs and into Miss Harper's room. I shut the door behind me. I walked over to her dresser and saw her beautiful silver hairbrush. It was inscribed with her initials in a beautiful sweeping calligraphy. I gently traced my fingers along its intricate filigree pattern. As I did, I saw my engagement ring and wedding band. I held my left hand out in front of me for several moments. My hands were shaking as I slid the rings off my finger. I felt as though I was amputating part of my body as I took them off. I held them for a few moments before gently setting them on the silver tray. Then, I walked over to the window seat to cry. I was so confused. Crying can be exhausting and after several minutes, I lay on the window seat, emotionally spent and wanting to sleep. I heard a knock on the door. I knew it had to be Trevor. He was the only one there.

"Come in," I said. I sat up, wiping my eyes, not that he wouldn't know I'd been crying. I didn't look at him as he entered the room and sat next to me on the window seat. He didn't say anything, but he made himself comfortable on the velvet cushions and waited for me to say something.

"I guess you're ready for your sous chef?"

I glanced up at him.

"Please don't shut me out, Grace."

I pushed the hair back from my face as I gathered my thoughts.

"I don't know where to begin."

"Wherever you need to."

That sounded simple enough. Where did I need to start? I noticed he was staring at my hand. I thought I saw the hint of a smile. He said nothing, but I knew he'd seen my bare fingers. I wasn't sure why I'd done that. It just felt like the right thing to do.

"I've just been thinking about the phone call, the last time I saw him in person, and my questioning this morning. He kept saying he didn't want to do this, but he had to."

"Is that the reason you took your rings off?"

My head dropped as I looked at my bare hands.

"He doesn't want me anymore. I guess I just need to get used to that idea."

I could feel the tears again. Was this ever going to end? I was tired of the pain, tired of crying.

"And yet, you still want to help him," Trevor whispered.

I met his gaze.

"You don't understand. I don't want to help him," I emphasized the word "want." It

wasn't a want. "I feel compelled to help him. I must help him, and I promised him I would although I had no idea of what I was saying at the time."

"No, you don't have to help him."

Trevor's voice was firm. He seemed to be trying to restrain his anger. I noticed his eye twitch. I reached out and touched his hand.

"That's the thing. I do have to help him. No one else is going to. If my dream is right, they have iron-clad evidence and fake witnesses. I don't know what's going on, but I'm sure that he's being set up."

"What else did he say in the message?"

"It was short. Two things I don't understand. He told me to tell Zack he had a great right hook and he told me not to forget to pay the mortgage. But the things I did understand were him calling me 'Gracie' and 'babe.' He called me 'Gracie' as a way of saying 'I'll take care of you.' So, whatever is going on, he's trying to shield me from something, or he was. And he told me to remember the things he'd said the last time we saw each other. On that day, he kept telling me to trust my instincts and to believe in my dreams."

I took a deep breath and let it out slowly.

Trevor didn't say anything.

"I can go back to my house now. I don't – "

"No, stay. Please."

I didn't know what to say.

"I don't want to impose."

"You're not imposing."

"Thank you for caring, Trevor."

"Grace, I care about you more than you realize."

I left that comment alone. It made me uncomfortable for some reason, and I glanced away.

"Someone in the department is setting him up. I just know it. I can't let an innocent man stay in jail and get wrongly convicted. I turned in one of my best friends a couple of months ago because I couldn't let an innocent man go to jail. I sent a woman with a baby to jail because I knew you didn't do something my hus-, ex-husband – said he had evidence you did."

He looked at me. I could tell he wasn't happy.

"And Dana is doing just fine, Grace," he said "She's out on bond, and she'll probably get a plea deal. She's not going to prison. Plenty of people agreed to step forward and testify on her behalf that Bill had abused her – emotionally and in other ways. She didn't come to the funeral because she didn't want the stares. We understand that, don't we?"

"Yes. I need to check on her."

"Maybe, but you don't have to do that today. You've been through enough."

He quickly changed the subject.

"Here's the reason for our dinner party tonight," he said. "Emmie's got connections at the FBI and Butch is your insider at the sheriff's department. Maybe you can sort this out with them. Look, I may not understand why you're trying to help him, but I've already told you that I would help you in any way I can."

"Thank you, Trevor."

"Let's go cut up some vegetables."

I followed him down the staircase and into the kitchen.

I grabbed a knife and bell pepper and started to slice it. He didn't say anything. The entire time I was in the kitchen working as his sous chef, preparing the vegetables for his beef bourguignon, there was silence. The rest of the meal would include a salad and a vegetable medley. I chopped more vegetables for that. There was no need to prepare desserts because we still had plenty. As I was cutting the last tomato for the salad, the doorbell rang. Trevor had left the kitchen a long time before as his dish simmered. I hadn't really noticed. I was painfully slow at cutting vegetables and in my own world trying to figure out what Drew was trying to tell me. It made no sense. I heard Trevor as he made his way across the heart pine floors. And then I heard a familiar voice.

"Dr. Trevor, could I see Miss Grace?"

"Of course, Jazzy, but you can just call me 'Trevor.' You know that, right?"

"Nope, I have to respect my elders."

"Jazzy, I'm not that old."

"You're still older than me, shug," she said.

I walked into the foyer, and Jazzy made a path straight toward me. She gave me a huge hug.

"Miss Beth sent me over here with a whole passel of flowers and stuff to make some arrangements."

"Really, now."

I folded my arms against my chest. Beth did have a strong sense of leadership. That's what we always said when she took over things, which was most of the time. It was kinder than calling her "bossy," which is what Emmie and I said in private.

"Yes, ma'am. She said just because you weren't at the shop didn't excuse you from working."

"I thought I owned the shop."

"You know how she can be, shug. We have a couple of weddings this weekend."

"Yes, I'm the one who booked those."

"And someone came in with a large order for a party this weekend."

"That sounds encouraging."

"There's lots of stuff going on."

I followed Jazzy outside. She was in Beth's vehicle not the shop's delivery van. I glanced at Trevor.

"Where can I set up shop?"

"I'm finished in the kitchen," he said. "The island is big enough, don't you think?"

"Yes, that's perfect."

He helped us bring in the flowers, containers, and everything else we needed to make the arrangements.

"I'm supposed to stay here with you until we're finished then take everything in."

"That sounds fine to me."

It took a little while to get everything set up and in order the way I liked it. Jazzy didn't say much during that time, which was odd because Jazzy chatted all the time.

"What's the matter, Jazzy?"

She looked a little shocked. She glanced around the room and then at me.

"Why do you say that?"

"Because you're so quiet."

She took a deep breath and let it out slowly.

"I appreciate everything y'all are doing for me."

"But?"

"It's not really a 'but.'"

"Yes, it is, Jazzy."

"Well, it's Miss Beth."

I laughed.

"She's kinda controlling."

"Just kind of?"

"Well, very."

"Okay, what's the matter?"

"It's not that I don't appreciate this."

"You already said that."

"I have a place to live. I'm not out on the streets. I'm not having —"

She paused and looked at me.

"Well you know. I don't like to think about what I had to do."

"I know, and we don't want you to have to do that anymore."

"I thought I'd be doing that all my life. I never thought I'd be free, but look at me. I'm going to school, and I even go to a therapist. Never would've thought that."

"So what's the matter?"

"I've never done what I want with my own life. Everybody's always told me what to do, where to live, what to be."

I smiled. I thought about Trevor. It seems like a lot of people were taking control of their lives these days.

"I don't think I want to do medical stuff. I mean, I know that there's lots of jobs here and good money, but I want to be creative. I love working in your shop, and I really think I want to do hair and nails."

"Jazzy, I think you'd be fantastic at that, and the world definitely needs people who can do that sort of thing. You're a natural. I'll talk to Beth. I totally understand where you're coming from with the medical thing. I went to school to be a nurse at first."

I paused. My heart ached for a moment. It was after passing out in biology class that I realized nursing was out. Then that same afternoon I had my minor fender bender that brought Deputy Drew Ward into my life. My life forever changed in one afternoon. No medical field for me - and Drew.

"Are you all right?" Jazzy asked me.

I gave her a weak smile.

"No, but I will be."

Jazzy paused for a few moments.

"I still need your help."

"That's what we're here for."

"Y'all have been so nice to me. I was talking to my therapist, and she said I was inspiring. She said I might like to volunteer, so I am. That's what I've been doing on my days off. I started at a senior center about a month ago, but I really want to work with kids."

I smiled.

"I don't have a record. I never got arrested, and your husband didn't take me in either."

"That's not what I was thinking. I was thinking that I'm proud of you."

I put down the flowers and gave her a hug.

"I sort of feel like you and Miss Beth and Miss Emmie are like my mamas."

"I consider that a compliment."

"You should. And I love your mama too. It's almost like having a grandma again. Ms. Lottie is amazing, and I love her lemon cakes."

"You and the rest of Augusta. What are you doing at the senior center?"

"What I do best. I talk; they talk, and we have fun. Being around them reminds me of being with my grandmama. I miss her so much. Sometimes kids from a nearby center come after school, and the seniors read to the little ones and talk. It's cool. Maybe I can tell older kids about my life someday and keep them from ever getting into trouble."

"Jazzy, I think that would be great."

Tears started forming in my eyes. I wasn't sure why. Jazzy made me want to be a better person. I wanted to be the person she thought I was. I didn't think she'd noticed, but Jazzy came to my side of the table and gave me a hug.

"What do you always tell me, Grace? Everything's going to be okay. I know it," she said softly.

Then she stepped back and put her hands on her hips.

"And I can't call you just 'Grace.' It feels wrong."

I laughed at that last comment because I repeatedly had asked her not to call me "Miss Grace." It was okay that my mother be "Miss Lottie," or Trevor's mom be "Miss Harper," but I thought I was too young for that designation just yet. Jazzy was only in her early 20s so I guess Beth, Emmie, and I were old women to her even though we were all only in our early 30s. I didn't say anything about what was on my mind. I didn't want to cry. I listened to the sound of Jazzy's voice. I didn't really hear the words she was saying. I was lost in trying to figure out what Drew was trying to tell me about the mortgage. I sent my brother a text asking him to call me when he was able.

Putting together the flowers was good for me. I needed to release all my feelings in a creative way because crying wasn't doing its job. Jazzy had left, and there was still time before Emmie and Butch were scheduled to arrive.

I wasn't sure where Trevor had disappeared to. I guess he was right about being able to live in this house and not run into anyone for several days. He probably needed time alone anyway. The lower level smelled incredible, and I knew dinner would taste as wonderful as it smelled.

I decided to sit on the upstairs porch. It was peaceful as a soft rain fell. I could see the remains of the gardens. I'd love to get my hands into that soil. Oh, the roses she once had. I wondered what else was down there.

As I was contemplating flowers, Zack called me.

"Hello, big brother."

"Hello, little sis. Where are you?"

"Why are you asking me that?"

"Just what I thought."

"What's that supposed to mean?"

"You aren't at the shop, and you weren't home last night."

"How did you know? I slept in one of the empty bedrooms at Trevor's house. Emmie and Trevor were worried about me staying home after they – we – heard about Drew. And it's not what you think."

"I'm not judging you, and I didn't imply anything. That's on you."

"Well, have a little faith in me. This place is huge. I think he's here, but I haven't seen him in a couple of hours. I didn't ask you to call to get lectured. That's the reason I haven't called Mama. I knew she'd be upset."

"No, she's upset because you haven't called her. She's been worried."

"I know. She worries about everything. Zack, tell her I'm fine. Just do it for me. It's been a rough few days with Trevor's mother's death, my divorce being final, and then Drew being arrested."

"Whoa, whoa, sis. Back up. Did you say 'divorce?'"

"Yeah, you knew that Drew filed, didn't you?"

"Well, I knew he'd talked about it, but no one has told me that you had actually filed."

"Okay so now you know. Drew and I are divorced. And that was another place I didn't want to go so that's why I'm at Trevor's."

"Grace, why didn't you tell us?"

"I don't want you feeling sorry for me. I already feel like the disappointing member of the Burke family."

"Gracie. I'm so sorry this has happened to you, but I don't feel sorry for you. There's a big difference."

"It's not your fault. You tried to help him – you tried to help me. It doesn't matter. What matters is that he's in jail, and I don't believe he did it. I think someone is framing him – maybe even someone in the sheriff's department."

"Whoa, sis. I've heard the news, but are you sure about the last part?"

"I've been hiding from reporters just in case. I went to the sheriff's office today, and they questioned me. Yesterday in all the confusion with the funeral, I missed Drew's phone call. He made his one call to me. I guess it was his call. I'm not sure where it came from or when he left the message. I only had a voice mail. It was strange."

"Oh, Gracie."

"Yes, I feel horrible, and he said some cryptic things that I don't understand."

"Okay. Is that why you wanted me to call you?"

"Yeah, he told me that I needed to tell Zack he has a great right hook?"

I heard him take a deep breath, and he paused so long I thought the call had dropped.

"You may be right, Gracie."

"Right about what?"

"Right about the fact that someone is setting him up."

Now it was my turn for a deep breath.

"So, what did he mean?"

"Well, I'm your brother. You've heard the expression 'brothers in arms,' right?"

"Yes."

"Well, the military and law enforcement sometimes refer to their line of work as a brotherhood. There's a bond that only people who've been in that line of work can understand. For him to tell you to tell me I have a great right hook says to me that whoever hooked him on this murder charge is someone he considers part of that brotherhood."

"Okay."

"And the hook. He and I used to go fishing some. How do you catch a fish? You bait a hook and you snare someone. He's in a big mess, sis. What else did he say?"

"The last time I saw him at our divorce hearing, he told me that he didn't trust anyone he worked with."

"Then, he definitely thinks someone is dirty. Anything else?"

"Yeah, he told me not to forget to pay the mortgage. I don't understand. But he also told me that I needed to remember the last thing he said to me about his cases. And the last thing he said was at our divorce hearing. He told me to trust my instincts and my dreams. He told me that he might need my help, but it would only be after he'd exhausted every lead."

Zack paused.

"Gracie, I have nothing on that one."

"It's okay. I'm coming up blank too. He's given me money the past couple of months for his part of the mortgage."

"Listen, I'm sorry I couldn't help him, but you can't help

someone who doesn't want to be helped, Gracie."

"Zack, I'm not blaming you. You were there for him. You tried to get him to get treatment. He came back from your trip to take him to the rehabilitation center in North Carolina in October and was so angry with me because I'd destroyed the first set of divorce papers. He printed another set and practically forced me to sign them," I paused. "I just wasn't enough for him."

"Don't be so hard on yourself. I know you tried. I know you gave it your all. None of us blame you for this."

"Now that you know, I guess I'll have to call Mama and Daddy. I just can't do it right now. This week has been so hard. And Trevor – he and I aren't – "

"Grace, the last thing I want to know about is my sister's private life. That's between you and whoever. It's not my business unless that man becomes a threat to you. Okay?"

"Thank you."

"No problem, but you need to tell Mama and Daddy. I'd leave out the part about you spending the night at Trevor's even if you have been sleeping in another room."

"I will. I just can't tonight. Trevor's actually been really good about giving me some space. And you understand I need alone time."

"I do, sis. Call me if you need me."

I had put Deputy Steed's card in my pocket. I stared at it for several minutes. I wondered why he gave it to me. I figured I'd find out. Maybe he could answer some questions that would help me get to the bottom of all of this.

"This is Steed," he answered.

I hesitated and almost hung up.

"Hi. This is Grace Ward."

"I'm glad you called me."

"Why?"

"You don't need to worry about Drew. I've seen him. He's pretty shaken, but he's physically okay. He has some scrapes, but he's good."

"But I am worried about him."

"I know, and he told me to tell you everything's going to be okay."

I wanted to cry now. It was on the tip of my tongue to tell him Drew had called me, but I wondered if he'd really seen Drew. Why did that thought pop into my head? Drew told me not to trust anyone. Now, I was paranoid. Why did this deputy want to reach out to me?

"Drew didn't do this."

"If there's evidence, we'll find it."

If – I didn't like that word.

"If? You don't sound too comforting."

"We're working on it and doing everything we can."

"What does that mean?"

"It means that you don't need to worry."

"But I am worried. He's accused of something I know he didn't do."

"Ma'am, you need to be careful of what you're saying."

I wasn't sure what he was implying by that.

"What do you mean?"

"I can't say anymore. But you don't need to try and solve this. You should stick to flowers and leave the police work to the professionals. Or else you could get hurt."

It wasn't the words, but it was his condescending tone. He was harsh – worse than Drew ever sounded. I wondered if that was a threat?

"How could I get hurt?"

He paused.

"Just take my word for it, and drop it, Mrs. Ward. You can get in too deep, too fast."

"Thank you for your time, Deputy Steed. I'll keep that in mind," I said as I ended the call without allowing him to say anything else. My hands were shaking as I put down the phone. It could've been a threat; maybe it was just a warning. Drew had me paranoid.

I couldn't shake the last conversation he and I had. He didn't trust anyone, and anyone I talked to could've done this to him. If my dream was right, then someone staged this whole thing – someone in the department with him. Why would someone set him up? But none of this was getting me any closer to finding out who did this.

"Drew, how am I supposed to help you?" I whispered the words in desperation. I felt like crying again just out of sheer frustration, but I didn't want to any more. I wanted to get past all these stupid tears.

I wondered about this woman Drew supposedly killed. I wondered how they ended up in that warehouse. My mind was racing to figure out how I was going to help Drew, but my thoughts were quickly interrupted by the sound of Trevor's voice.

"You really seem to enjoy my porches," he said.

I turned to look at him. He was wearing a pair of gray trousers and a white long-sleeve shirt which was rolled to three-quarters' length. In his hand were three pink roses wrapped in white tulle. My heart skipped, and I smiled.

"I've always loved porches. My parents' house has one, and some of the best memories of my life have taken place on a porch swing. When Drew and I bought our house, the thing that called to us was the front porch. We used to spend so much time there, but as time passed, we stopped. I'm not sure what happened."

He sat down next to me. I felt like a mess in yoga pants and a T-shirt. He smiled at me.

"I had a few good memories of sitting on your parents' front porch. We laughed many nights there."

I didn't say much.

"Why are you so dressed up?"

"Dinner guests. Mama always taught me to dress appropriately for dinner guests."

He held the flowers out to me. As most people know roses say many things, especially when it comes to color. Pink roses mean a lot of things. In general, pink roses mean 'grace.' I guess that was fitting since it was my name, but I looked closer at the roses; there were three shades of pink in the bouquet. The light pink meant gentleness or that you admired someone; the medium shade is often given to a first love or to cheer someone who is grieving; and the dark pink expressed gratitude. And all of those things had to do with our current situation.

I took them from him. I knew that Jazzy had put them together. There was a light dusting of glitter on the tulle and a slender, sequined ribbon intertwined with the others. Jazzy loved glitter and sparkle, and I felt her winking at me. She knew who this was for.

"Thank you."

"A very animated young woman told me about the meanings of the colors, and they say everything I can't."

"They are actually perfect, Trevor. Perfect."

"You once told me you didn't get many flowers."

I gave a weak smile.

"Hazard of the job, I suppose."

"Would you go to Columbia with me to see the Nutcracker this weekend?"

Augusta had a couple of ballet companies that performed the Nutcracker each year. One performed Thanksgiving weekend; there was even an African-American, Southern version of the Nutcracker performed to jazz renditions of Tchaikovsky's music by Duke Ellington, but they'd all passed because it was getting so close to Christmas. Columbia, South Carolina was only about an hour away. Christmas – I kept trying to forget it was almost Christmas. It wasn't the most wonderful time of the year this year.

"I'd love to."

He smiled.

"I have orchestra seats, so we should be close to the stage."

"Are you sure you're up for the Nutcracker? I think we saw at least 20 different versions of it online."

He laughed.

"We saw some interesting ones, didn't we, Grace?"

"Yes, we did."

"My mother wanted me to take you, and I want to honor her memory that way."

I smelled the roses. I loved the feel of the soft petals as they grazed my face.

"I have some vases downstairs if you'd like to put them in water."

"You have a ton of vases downstairs. I should know. I think you got many of them from my shop recently."

"I'm doing my best to support local businesses."

"Trevor, what are your plans now that…"

"I'm still deciding on what I'm going to do. I know what I'd like to do, and I have a few offers. I do know I'm not going back to the oncology group in Charlotte. Beyond that, I'm not making any decisions until after the first of the year. I'm going to rest and help you solve a case."

I smiled.

"Thank you, Trevor, but I don't even know where to start."

He caught my gaze.

"I think you do, Grace. Just don't overthink it. Go with your instincts."

"I don't think my instincts are all that great. I'm not a good judge of character."

"Because you care too much."

"Maybe. I guess I should change for dinner. I'm very underdressed."

4

Emmie and Butch showed up right on time.

Everything smelled incredible, but I wasn't hungry. I was anxious. I had a nervous knot in the pit of my stomach.

"Where are the boys? I never get to see them anymore, Emmie."

"Their soccer team had some holiday get-together tonight and I forgot about it. I switched days with their dad. It probably worked out better anyway."

This was always the awkward part for me. The part where the guests arrived, but you couldn't just rush to the table to eat. There had to be small talk. And it seemed even more awkward because Butch and Emmie were obviously a couple, but Trevor and I were not.

"Trevor, I brought a bottle of red wine; Grace, can I help you do anything?"

Emmie knew I wasn't good with this. She always gave me an exit strategy.

"It's Trevor's kitchen."

"If you two would like to go in the other room and talk about us, that's fine with me," Trevor said.

We headed to the kitchen, and Emmie put the bottle in the refrigerator.

"So, the two of you?"

She smiled, and I glared at her.

"Nothing has changed since last night."

"Oh really. You were wearing those wedding rings yesterday. Something either happened with Drew or Trevor, and I'd prefer to think it was Trevor. God, those eyes, I could get lost there."

She winked at me.

"What about Butch?"

Emmie broke my glance as she looked at the floor then she took quick peeks around her as if she was looking for someone. She moved close to me and lowered her voice.

"I'm probably going to break up with him after Christmas."

"Why?"

"He wants to move in with me, and that's not happening. I don't want him upsetting my life and the boys," she paused and looked around to make sure he wasn't coming in the room. She lowered her voice. "I don't know there's just something I can't put my finger on. Besides, I don't know if I'm ready."

"You've been divorced for four years, and you're not ready. But I've been divorced 48 hours and that makes me ready?"

"No, but it's not just about me. I have to think of the boys. Butch has some great qualities, but I'm not sure he's ready to be a dad. And in the past week or so, he's really been on edge. I've seen him get angry over the slightest things, and he's really been jumpy. He's so different."

She moved away.

"But I can't do it a week before Christmas."

I didn't know what to say to that. I'd gotten a final divorce decree so close to Christmas. I glanced away and heard her gasp.

"Oh Grace, I'm sorry. I didn't mean – "

"It's okay, Emmie."

"No, it's not, but you seem different today."

"It's been a busy 24 hours. I had a message from Drew. He called, and I missed it. I don't know what was going on, but I missed it."

"Oh, honey. Yesterday was full. I know you didn't ignore it."

"But he doesn't know that."

She reached out and hugged me.

"What else?"

"Well, I had a dream about Drew; I was questioned by the police and I had a short phone call with another deputy."

"I guess I'll find out about all of that later."

"Yes."

"That outfit you have on looks cute, by the way. You have excellent taste."

I'd changed out of the yoga pants into a pair of slacks and muted silver sweater that Emmie had bought. I was wearing my black pumps.

"Thank you, Emmie. You did a great job, but I hate to think of how much I owe Trevor."

"I think I heard him say the words 'Christmas present.'"

"Fine, but it's too expensive of a Christmas present."

She touched my arm.

"Usually, Beth is 'that' friend – the blunt one."

"Oh, you think so? I'm surrounded by them."

"Okay, I can be the blunt friend too. Grace, let Drew go. He walked out on you. He wouldn't get help for his drinking problem. He wouldn't stick with counseling. He hasn't called or texted or anything except now when he wants you to possibly put your life in danger for him. Let him go," Emmie said sharply.

"After I clear his name, I'll let him go, but not until then. You and I both know that he's innocent."

I could match her sharp tone.

"Grace, you're playing with fire."

"No, Emmie. I'm not. I don't know how to solve crimes. I just arrange flowers, but I know I have to save Drew. Can't you see someone is trying to ruin him? Do you honestly believe that he killed someone? Cold-blooded killing?"

"Grace, he's got a serious drinking problem, and you know it. He probably doesn't even remember what happened that night."

"It doesn't mean he killed someone. I'd bet my very life on it."
Emmie folded her arms against her chest and shook her head.

"Okay, Grace. I give up. I can see there's no arguing with you.
I've seen this side of you before, and it's stubborn."

"Yes, you'll lose this one, Emmie. You need to be the one to
let it go."

I ended the conversation there. It wasn't my house, and I
didn't think it was my dinner party, but I tried to play the role of
hostess as best I could. While the Blake home had a formal dining
room, we ate in the breakfast nook. It was cozy. And by cozy, I'm
meant cramped. We were all too close for my liking especially with
the tension in the room. I felt like I was suffocating. Emmie had
already expressed how she felt about Drew, and I was concerned
about discussing my suspicions that someone from the department
was in on this. I really did not want to talk about my phone call from
Drew. Trevor sat next to me with Emmie and Butch across from us
at the cramped table. Emmie could command a room, and I let her
have it. She and Trevor kept the conversation going for most of the
meal. I have no idea what they talked about. But we all knew we were
dancing around the real reason we'd gathered. The food was delicious,
but I only had a few bites. I'm glad Trevor had resorted to gourmet
cooking as therapy for the stresses of his job. It obviously worked for
him. I knew I could never make meals like this one.

I was lost in thought as usual when Emmie finally addressed
the elephant in the room.

"So, Grace, would you like to tell us why we're here or not?"

I looked at her. We'd gone through all the pleasantries, and I
was long past being bored with it all.

"How about I opt for the 'or not' part?"

Emmie rolled her eyes.

"I've waited long enough for you to tell me about what's
going on," she said.

I stared at Butch.

"Drew kept me out of his work life. What does everyone in

the department think of this?"

"Everyone, as in?"

"The people he worked with – other deputies."

"They're all as shocked as I am. Drew is – was – a great officer."

"What about innocent until proven guilty, Butch?"

"Grace, it doesn't look good for him."

"And you can't tell me anything."

"No, I can't."

I was starting to raise my voice. I was getting agitated. I took a deep breath.

"Trevor, did you make dessert? I thought there was something chocolate in the fridge."

He looked puzzled.

"There's all kinds of desserts left over from what people brought after the funeral."

I started to get up.

"We don't need dessert, Grace. What did he say to you?" Emmie asked.

I settled back into my seat. Emmie and Butch were staring intently.

"Wait a minute. You talked to Drew?" Butch seemed confused.

"I had a voicemail message from him. I think I was his phone call, or he called me before he was arrested. I'm not sure."

Butch's mouth dropped.

"Did Drew have enemies, Butch?" I asked.

"Of course, he did. How many people has he put behind bars?"

"A lot. But was there anyone specific you knew who might have –" I paused as I struggled with my thoughts. "Did he have enemies in the department?"

I don't like where you're going with this, Grace," he snapped. "There were a couple of people who weren't happy that he got promoted especially after what had happened with Mark and Linda. Are you happy now, Grace? One was Mitch Colley and the other was Patrick Steed, who was so nice to your face today. Neither of them thought he should be promoted. They both wanted the job and felt they were more qualified. Do you want to question them? Do you want to accuse them to their faces? Patrick gave you his number. Why don't you call him?

I didn't respond. I wasn't going to tell him that I'd spoken with Deputy Steed.

"You're treading on thin ice with me, Grace. I don't care if you were married to Drew. I can see why he left you. You meddle in everything," he said as he threw his napkin onto the table and stood up. "How dare you accuse my brothers of doing something to him? We're all upset about this, but not for one second do I think it's anyone I work with. No one would do this to Drew. Everything points to him doing it himself."

"Deputy Childress, I think you need to leave. Now," I could hear Trevor saying. I felt his hand resting on my shoulder; I was vaguely aware that he'd stood up too. I looked down at the plate. It had tasted wonderful, but I'd barely touched it. I'd ruined everything.

"Are you ready?" Butch growled at Emmie.

"I'm not going anywhere with you, Butch. Grace is my best friend, and if she believes that someone is setting up Drew, I believe her too. And I won't tolerate anyone treating her that way. You've got brothers; she's my sister."

"Fine, I guess you and I are done too."

I glanced up to see Emmie staring at me. His words punched me in the chest; they took my breath away. What was I going to do? He was one of the few people I thought could help me.

I heard the door close. There was no way to slam a door as heavy as the front door of the Blake house. Trevor must have followed him to lock the door because I didn't feel the weight of his hand on my shoulder.

"I'm sorry, Emmie," I whispered.

"No, Grace, you just saved me a huge headache. Now I don't have to wait until after Christmas to break up with him. Like I said, he's been acting erratic, and I don't know why. He's also been angry. I thought it was Drew rubbing off on him. He had been drinking more than he usually does. Now, will you please tell me what's going on?"

As I relayed to her my conversations with Drew, Zack, and Deputy Steed, Trevor sat back down next to me. He put a reassuring hand on my arm. Emmie listened without saying anything. She kept my gaze the entire time.

"This is a mess, Grace."

"I don't know who I can trust, and I really don't know too many people. Drew really did keep that part of his life to himself. He didn't want me involved. Mark and Butch are the only people I ever spent much time with on a regular basis. I know some people by name. I had met Capt. Howard and Deputy Steed before today. I didn't get to know them. Anytime I'd seen them before was just small talk, and you know how good I am at that. I remember meeting Mitch one time. His biceps were bigger than my thighs. He could've entered a bodybuilding contest. And he was so smug. He reminded me a lot of Bill Andrews. I didn't like the way Patrick Steed talked to me today. I felt like he might've been threatening me."

"Yeah, I met them too. They are friends of Butch," Emmie said.

"Really?"

"Yes, we went out with Mitch and his girlfriend. She's like 10 years younger than him. She's cute. Anyway, he made some snide comments about Drew, talking about how he should've had that job. He said that Drew was fake. Drew pretended to like the higher-ups, and that he shouldn't have been promoted. He droned on and on about how wonderful he was. I finally excused myself to the ladies' room for a long time. His girlfriend followed me in to the restroom. She acted skittish when I asked about the two of them. My gut told me that something wasn't right, but I couldn't put my finger on it. And I did meet Patrick. He was quiet. He never mentioned Drew. In fact, I think it was his girlfriend who talked all night. And boy did she talk. She was the one who said he should've been promoted but wasn't. He shushed her. He didn't want to talk about it."

"You know what they say about the quiet ones. He seemed really nice today until I called him. Then, he sounded like Drew on repeat – leave this to the professionals, and if we get evidence, we'll clear him. Not, we will find that evidence to clear him."

"We'll figure it out, but I think the first thing is to decipher what that whole mortgage thing means."

"Yeah, I know."

"Not to cut this evening short. Take as much time as you'd like, but I can take you home, Emmie, whenever you're ready. Unless you want to chaperone us," Trevor interjected.

Emmie grinned at me.

"Only if I can be like the matchmaker in The Quiet Man. I loved that movie. I can oversee your courtship."

I shook my head.

"Dinner was wonderful, Trevor. I'm sorry I ruined everything."

"Does she do this all the time, Emmie?"

"Apologize? Yes, all the time, Trevor, all the time."

"She didn't always do that, did she?"

They weren't even looking at me while they carried on their conversation.

"Why are you talking about me like I'm not even here?" I was frustrated now. Emmie caught my eye and stared at me.

"No, she wasn't. It's only been in the past year or two," she said with her eyes never leaving me.

I started to apologize for that too, but I knew the point they were trying to make.

"The next time I go see my therapist I'll talk to her about it. Is that okay with the two of you?"

"Grace, we care about you," Emmie said. "Honestly, I think you should let the professionals handle this one. You're too close to the situation. And I think you have some kind of guilt that makes you want to fix things with Drew – things that can't be fixed."

I stood up. I was done for the night. I picked up my plate and looked at Trevor.

"I really am sorry I ruined the night, and I might be your guest, but I'm cleaning the dishes."

I walked to the kitchen and began rinsing off the plates to put into the dishwasher. Emmie was close on my heels.

"Grace, I'm sorry."

"Emmie, you've said enough. Please just leave me alone. If everyone is like Butch and Patrick, then Drew is doomed.".

Trevor brought in several dishes from the table.

"And there is plenty of dessert if anyone wants some," he added.

Chocolate always diffused any fights I'd ever had with Emmie. Neither of us could resist its charm. Trevor went over to the counter.

"Let's see. This chocolate cake is from Mrs. Davis. I think it was a little dry. There's some amazing lemon pound cake baked by Grace's mom."

"You're hoarding your mom's lemon pound cake, and you didn't offer me a slice, Grace. I'm hurt. Where's a plate?" Emmie asked.

My mother had made lemon pound cake. She brought it by at some point before the funeral, but she didn't stay long. She'd given me a hug and a peck on the cheek and hightailed it out. She wasn't one for too many social occasions. For funerals, however, my mother was going to make her pound cake. And for this one, I think she made macaroni and cheese too.

"Emmie, there's some mac and cheese too that she made if you want to take it to the boys."

"That would be heavenly."

Trevor sliced two pieces of cake.

"Do you want some, Grace?"

"You wouldn't happen to have any milk, would you?"

"Of course."

Milk and my mother's pound cake – the first comfort food in my life. And once again a tense situation had been avoided and without chocolate. My mother's pound cake beat chocolate any day of the week.

"I'm sorry about Butch, Emmie."

"You've already said that. Stop apologizing. He showed me what I needed to see, and like I said, I was going to break up with him after Christmas anyway. I'm glad I hadn't gone out and bought him a present."

She made me laugh. With the three of us, it took little time to clean off the table and devour the remainder of my mother's cake.

"Grace, I'd forgotten how mouth-watering your mother's cake is. Do you know her secrets?" asked Trevor.

I shook my head.

"Sorry, but the baking gene missed this generation."

"How is it possible for this cake to get better?" Emmie asked as she placed a bite in her mouth.

"That's her pride and joy. She has tweaked that thing over the years countless times, and my dad is always the willing guinea pig."

"Well, Trevor, we've let you in on our little secret," Emmie turned and looked at him. "Sugar has gotten us through two divorces and three murders. Caffeine helps, but only if it's in chocolate. We like chocolate best unless Miss Lottie's pound cake is around."

He smiled as Emmie continued.

"So, if you're ever in the doghouse with her, chocolate will go a long way. Most men do the whole flowers thing, but chocolate is a much better substitute. It will go much further. Speaking of doghouses, Grace, Jimmy Hughes came in this morning."

I smiled.

"He asked about you. He said he's been worried about you since he'd heard about Drew leaving. He bought a bunch of flowers for Peggy. I made something amazing for her."

"You always do. What was his transgression this time?"

"He bought another antique gun."

"He said if you need anything, he knew a good lawyer and he'd be willing to help Drew in any way he could."

"That's sweet of him. I don't know if Drew has a lawyer at all." I pushed the cake away.

"Grace, I didn't mean to upset you."

"Emmie, it doesn't take much right now. Look, I really need to be alone even though I love both of your company. I just can't do this anymore today."

I searched both of their faces, hoping they'd just let me slip away. Emmie hugged me tightly as Trevor put his hand on my shoulder.

I broke away and rushed up the stairs into the solitude of the Victorian-inspired room. I slipped into yoga pants, a T-shirt and threw my hair into a pony tail. I was done for the night. How was I supposed to help Drew? There were only three people in the sheriff's department I'd had any contact with. And I wasn't sure I could trust any of them. Plus, they kept saying that I needed to leave things to the professionals. I took that to mean they weren't interested in my help. I sat on the window seat, and that's where I fell asleep. I was too tired to fight sleep, too emotionally drained. And I should've known that dreams would overtake me.

In this dream, I was in the jail, visiting Drew, a window separating us. Wearing a bright orange jumpsuit, he had dark circles under his eyes. I noticed a couple of bruises on his face as if he'd been beaten. I picked up the phone and stared at him. He held the phone with one hand and he placed his other hand on the glass. I put mine there too.

"I know I shouldn't ask for your help, but you're the only person I trust, Grace. I'm sorry, but I need you to help me. You'll figure it out. All of it. I know you will. Call your mother."

I awoke with a jolt, but I wasn't on the window seat where I remembered falling asleep. I was in bed, surrounded by pillows. I had no idea what time it was. I looked around for my phone. It was on the bedside table. I didn't remember putting it there. 3:24 a.m. That sounded about right. I wished I had my dream journal with me. I'd put the paper with my other dream in my purse. I pulled the paper out to add this one to it. It was easy enough to remember. Now wide awake, I wasn't sure I could go back to sleep. The temperature was in the 50s. That wouldn't be too bad. I picked up the small blanket that was on the window seat and wrapped it around me while I sat on the swing.

I tried to figure out what could possibly be my next move. I had to figure out what he meant by paying the mortgage. I was wasting time. I did have a mortgage on the small building that was my business. I'd bought the former house for a song and turned it into a flower shop. It needed a lot of work initially. I learned early that there was only so much Drew could help me do. I paid to have the heavy stuff taken care of – plumbing, electrical, heating and air conditioning. But Emmie, Drew, and I rolled up our sleeves to paint the walls and put in floors.

I rocked in the swing as the wind began to howl. Numb – inside and outside. That's how I felt as I sat and looked at the stars twinkling in the early morning sky. I didn't stay outside long. Instead of worrying about Drew, I started to pray. It actually came easier this time. I couldn't do anything for him at 3 a.m. anyway. Worry was only going to rob my sleep, but prayer eased my mind and I slipped into another slumber.

5

I awoke to the sunlight streaming in the window. I really should go to the shop. It was ridiculous of me not to. I checked the time. 8 a.m. How did I sleep so late? I stared at my phone. There were several texts including almost identical ones from Beth and Emmie.

We've got the shop under control. You need to rest. And you can't help Drew from here. But if you feel the need to stop by, please do.

I put on a pair of jeans and a top and brushed my hair before going downstairs. I could smell something, and it smelled wonderful. If Trevor decided to become a chef, I think he'd do a great job of it. I walked into the kitchen. Trevor was wearing a T-shirt and a pair of sweatpants.

"I was beginning to wonder if I was going to have to have you resuscitated," he said, smiling and winking at me.

"Thank you for checking on me after you got home from taking Emmie."

"You were curled up in a ball in a position that looked so uncomfortable. You didn't even stir when I picked you up and put you into bed."

The morning light cut into the kitchen, glistening on his blonde locks. He glanced at me and that same light danced in his blue eyes. He'd caught me staring.

"Is something wrong, Grace?"

I quickly looked away. I was embarrassed.

"No, nothing."

"I made omelets and sweet tea since you don't drink coffee."

"You're going to spoil me."

He grinned at me and set two beautiful plates on the table. He poured orange juice into wine glasses.

"I can cook a little, Trevor."

"You're still a guest in my house, Grace, and I will take care of my role as host."

He sat down next to me.

Before he could say anything else, my phone started to ring. My heart sank. It was my mother. What was I going to tell her? I knew both of my parents had to be disappointed, and I hadn't called her in several days. I spoke to her briefly during the funeral, but I didn't say much.

"It's my mother," I said to Trevor.

I picked my phone up and walked out of the room before answering it.

"Hi, Mama."

"Grace, I know you're busy, but I got a Christmas card in the mail from someone who wasn't on my list. Naturally, I had to send them one. I put it in the mailbox this morning, and there was a brown envelope in there. It was postmarked a few days ago. It must've been put in the neighbor's box by mistake. I thought the handwriting looked familiar. When I opened the envelope, there was a note from Drew, and there was another envelope for you."

I took a deep breath.

"What did his note say?"

"I'll let you read it."

"Give me a couple of minutes, and I'll be there."

I ended the call and stared at my phone. What on earth could Drew have sent me?

"Is everything all right?"

I turned to see Trevor leaning against the door frame.

"Drew sent an envelope to my mother. She found it this morning."

"I guess I know what you're doing this morning. Please eat before you leave."

I nodded and followed him back into the kitchen. I needed to get in the right headspace before seeing my mother. I'd have to tell her I was divorced, and I wasn't ready. I couldn't exactly tell her I'd spent the past two nights at Trevor's house even though nothing had happened.

"You'll be fine."

"I haven't told her."

"I know, but she'll understand."

"You said you talked to her about us?"

"I stopped by one day, and I told both of your parents that I was apologizing for the rumors they were sure to be hearing about their daughter and me. I told them I didn't step back into your life until after he'd left you. They seemed concerned about you, but they believed me. They asked about my mother, and I told them about the flowers you were bringing to her. And then Miss Lottie sent home two slices of pound cake. She promised not to tell you I'd stopped by."

"That sounds like my mother."

"She's got more faith in you than you give her credit for."

"Thank you and thank you for breakfast."

"I can go with you if you'd like."

"That's sweet of you, but I think I'm going to do this one alone."

It was only about a 10-minute drive to my parents' house. I drove slowly. I wanted to read whatever Drew had sent me, but at the same time, I was nervous. I knew my parents loved me, but I'd always felt Zack had been their favorite. He was the soldier and hero with the wife and loving family. Now they lived in town and had the house with the white picket fence – no lie. I just didn't want to be the disappointment in their lives.

I pulled into their driveway, and my mother was outside, sweeping the walkway. No, she was waiting for me. Sweeping was just something to pass the time. My dad was on the porch reading the newspaper and drinking his coffee on this mild December morning. I took a deep breath before getting out of the car. I gave Mama a hug.

"How are you handling all of this?"

I shook my head.

"Why don't we go inside?"

I hugged my dad on the way inside the house. We went straight into the kitchen, the heart of my mother's home.

"I have pound cake," she said.

"I had some at – "

I stopped. Around some people my mouth ran ahead of my brain.

"I had dinner at Trevor's last night with Emmie and Butch, and there was pound cake for dessert – that you'd taken over after the funeral. Emmie said it gets better every time you make it."

"How's Trevor?"

"Exhausted. I don't think it's really hit him yet. He was Miss Harper's caregiver until her final hours. That's draining."

"He's such a nice young man," she said and smiled. "And how are you?"

"It's been one heck of a week. Before we go on, I have to tell you something. Drew and I filed for divorce, and it's been finalized. He and I aren't married anymore."

There I'd said it. It felt much better in a way. The weight was lifted at least.

"Oh Grace, why didn't you tell me?"

"Mama, I just don't want to cry right now. With Trevor's mother's illness and death, the divorce, and now Drew in jail and awaiting charges, I'm barely able to keep it altogether."

She nodded and got up from the table. She returned with an envelope. It was addressed to Gracie. Then, I could hear his words from my dream. "Call your mother."

"Do you mind if I read this alone?"

I looked up at her. She smiled, and I headed back out to the porch. My father had come back inside and was watching 24-hour news. I paused as I heard the announcer.

"A Georgia law enforcement officer has been charged with voluntary manslaughter in the death of a young woman. Vanessa Graham was found shot and killed earlier this week. Andrew David Ward, a 15-year veteran with Augusta's Richmond County Sheriff's Department is scheduled to be arraigned this morning."

My dad changed the channel after he heard me suck in that last breath. My hands were trembling as I went out to the porch and opened the letter.

Dear Grace,

By now, one of two things has happened. I'm either dead or I've been accused of something I can promise you I didn't do.

But first, please know that I never wanted to hurt you. Maybe one day I can explain it, but I can't now. Just know that I divorced you to protect you. I know it doesn't make sense to you. How could breaking your heart be protecting you? Like I said, I can't explain now because I feel like I'm undoing everything I tried to do.

I have no right to ask for your help. If you hate me, I understand, and I don't hold it against you. If you don't want to help me, I get it. But there are a handful of people who are bad news in this department. They are smart, and they cover their tracks very well. I've been putting together evidence. I don't know all of the details, and I don't know everyone who is involved. I wanted to have all my ducks in a row before I made any accusations. I'm close – too close. That's the reason I think – no, I know – something is going to happen. I just need a couple more pieces of evidence. I do have enough to get someone's interest though.

I've hidden some clues for you. You're smart; you'll figure it out. But they'll be in places I don't think other people will look.

I trust your instincts. You'd make a great investigator; maybe even better than me. Don't doubt yourself. I'm sorry I did.

Drew

Tears blurred my vision as I stared at the paper.

I didn't look up, but I felt my mother sit next to me on the swing. She put her arm around me, and I burst into tears. His letter only confused me the more. I had to figure this out. I sat up and wiped my eyes.

"I can't explain it. I still love Drew, but when I look at Trevor, I get so confused. My heart skips. He's so kind to me. He's gentle. He's too perfect. He even irons sweatpants. Who does that?"

"He's a man; he's not perfect," my mother responded dryly.

Her tone made me laugh.

"I know he's not, but what if he's actually a mass murderer hiding behind all that perfection? Maybe he really did kill Bill, like Drew implied, and maybe he's the one who framed Drew and got him thrown in jail. He could be behind Vanessa Graham's murder or whoever she was. He's got money. He could've hired someone and washed his hands of it."

"Now you're being ridiculous," she said.

"Well, I never thought Dana would kill Bill."

"Sometimes people do things in a split second that they never wanted to. And she still claims it was an accident. Besides, there's a difference in Dana and what you're suggesting. You're talking about pure, cold-blooded killing. Dana didn't do that. I believe she'd finally had enough of him, and she snapped."

"I want to believe her, but I can't imagine living with Bill. He was so arrogant and so cruel."

"Not worth planning out a murder though."

"No, but maybe planning it and making it look like an accident?"

"Do you really believe that?"

Part of me did. Part of me thought the whole accident excuse was simply that – a made up excuse.

"And I don't think Trevor is a serial killer, Grace. His mother taught him better than that."

I laughed. That was such a Lottie thing to say. She was right about Miss Harper teaching him well, but I don't think her mind was on keeping him from becoming a serial killer. She just wanted him to be polite and well-mannered.

"I don't either, Mama. You should've seen him with his mother. He was amazing to her."

"I'm sure he was. You care about him, don't you? That's the reason you're trying to talk yourself into believing he's a serial killer."

"He hurt me once already."

"He was only 19. He had a lot of growing up to do."

"I know, but I never thought Drew would leave me either."

"I know, honey. But I also know that Drew couldn't get rid of all those demons he was fighting. Your father and I know that you tried to go to counseling with him. Zack tried to step in and help you. Pastor B tried to help him. Drew quit trying. He let his troubles win. We watched it. We watched him quit on you. The past two years have been so hard for me to just watch and say nothing, Grace. With you losing the babies, then the murders and Drew, all I wanted to do was stop your pain. And then Trevor comes back into your life. I'll never forget that day he came here after you'd started dating Drew. When I told him, the look in his eyes told me everything. He was crushed and angry. We know that nothing happened between you and Trevor. Don't worry about what everyone else thinks."

"You sound just like Trevor."

"I think he's a good man. He just had to grow up."

"I think I'm – I don't know, Mama. I'm so confused."

I shook my head. I don't know why I had problems verbalizing my feelings. Mama just gave me an understanding smile and nodded.

"You love him?" she asked softly.

I stared at her.

"Yes? I don't know. I can't love him and Drew at the same time. How is that possible?"

"I don't know the answer to that, but eventually you will move on. Drew's not coming back, and you have to face that."

I knew she was right, and Emmie kept saying the same thing.

"You talked to Trevor?"

She touched my hands.

"I visited Miss Harper some during her illness. I took her cake because I heard from Mary Louise that she liked it, so yes, I've talked to Trevor a couple of times."

"He didn't tell me that."

"He told me that you were kind to him too. It sounds familiar. He said you listened to him, and you just let him be. You didn't want anything from him; you only offered support in spite of what you were going through. It seemed important to him – that you didn't want anything from him. He's a young doctor, and people expect a lot from him. They expect him to know all the answers, to make the right decisions, to be an authority, to work miracles. Some women view him as quite a catch, which he is, but you just let him be 'Trevor.'"

"He told you that?"

She nodded at me.

"He used those exact words. Do you think of Trevor as your friend?"

"Yes, I feel like I can tell him anything. Well, almost anything. I waited on the divorce because I was afraid he'd think – I don't know what I was afraid of. I guess I thought if he knew I wasn't married any longer, things would change. I don't know if I'm ready for things to change yet. I'm confused and scared."

"No one is saying you need to marry him tomorrow. Give it time, but don't dismiss him completely."

"What am I supposed to do about Drew?"

I handed her the letter and watched as she read it.

"Do you believe him, Grace?"

"I knew from the second I heard Robert Parnell reporting on it that it wasn't true. I know that Drew would never kill anyone unless his life was in danger or if he was protecting someone."

"Grace, I always taught you to fight for what and who you

believed in. Lord knows we had plenty of strays in this house, and they weren't the furry kinds either. Emmie and Beth seemed to have turned out okay, but when they were teenagers, they were something else. You've always been on the side of the person who was beaten and downtrodden. I think that's the main reason you are having such a hard time with Drew right now. You want to fix him, but you can't do that. "

"You're right on that."

"And I know you love him. You were married to him. But I also think you are looking at him through eyes of what used to be and not what is now. That can carry you through to help him, but you're eventually going to have to let that go too. He's not coming back to you, Grace."

I took a deep breath. I wondered if that was the reason I felt I had to help him. Did I want to save him and bring him back? Maybe.

"Yes, I know."

"And I think Trevor Blake could be good for you, especially now. But I'm not telling you to rush anything."

"Mama, Drew called me, and I missed it."

My mother's mouth dropped.

"And I've had two dreams about him. Our last face-to-face conversation was strange, and now this letter."

"What did he say?"

"In the dream, he told me to call you. In the phone message, he told me something about Zack, and he told me not to forget to pay the mortgage."

She wrinkled her mouth and tilted her head as she thought for a moment. Then she smiled.

"Do you remember when the shop was going through a rough patch a couple of years ago, and your dad and I paid the mortgage on the building for a couple of months?"

"Yes."

"Well, if he's hiding clues, remember the giant vase you gave me with the flowers to thank me?"

"Yes. You gave it back to me. It's at the shop, and it would be the perfect place to hide something. I hope you're right. I need to go. Thank you for everything."

I jumped back into my car and headed to my shop. I wondered if he'd hidden something there. There were plenty of nooks and crannies. I thought he'd given me my key back though. I could hear laughter and chattering when I walked through the back door, but it stopped immediately. I walked into the work room to see Beth, Emmie, and Jazzy all staring at me. I smiled and waved at them.

"You didn't have to stop on my account."

"What are you doing here?" Emmie queried.

"I missed you too, Emmie."

"It's not that we didn't miss you. We just thought you were laying low," Beth chimed in.

"I can't. I have a mystery to solve."

"You know he's being arraigned today."

"I heard it on the news. I went by my parents' house. All the more reason to figure this out."

I walked into the gift shop to find the vase. It was on a counter and it was heavy. I wanted to put it on the floor, so I could dismantle it easier. I started to lift it by myself when I felt a presence behind me. I turned around to see three sets of eyes boring holes into my back. Jazzy stepped up and helped me pull it down. When we set it on the floor, I moved the flowers out of the way, but I didn't see anything.

"Could I get two of you to pick this up, so I could look under it?"

Emmie and Jazzy stared at me. The base of the container was broad. As they lifted it up, I saw a small piece of paper attached to the underside. I pulled it off to read it.

Chew on this. Let our history be buried.

"What is it, Grace?" Emmie asked.

"A clue."

She raised an eyebrow.

"Okay," she said slowly, then she paused. "Grace, after Trevor took me home, Butch showed up."

I stared at her.

"Oh no. It's not what you think. I wasn't sure why he'd come. He gave me a lame apology, but I told him it was over. No one disrespects my sister and then waltzes right back into my life. I asked him about Patrick and Mitch."

I waited for her to continue.

"I was going to call you. Anyway, Butch said Mitch has had some disciplinary problems. He was reported about some illegal drug usage. He failed a random drug test, but he wiggled out of it somehow, saying he had a prescription for an opioid pain killer because of an injury. Butch said everyone has assumed that Drew was the tipster. I don't really have anything on Patrick except that Patrick didn't think Drew should've been cleared for duty so fast after Mark and Linda's death. Patrick and Mitch were both up for promotion the same time as Drew, and neither of them got promoted. There's been some bad blood. People know about Drew's drinking problem, and so Butch thinks that those two have it in for him."

"Oh, but I was just randomly accusing people," I snapped

"I know, honey. Trust me, I sent him away after I got the information, and he knows he's not welcome back. He's not going to treat my best friend that way."

"And to think I missed all the fun because I wasn't invited," Beth interjected.

'Trust me, it wasn't fun, and Butch wasn't nice," I said.

"No, you're right; he wasn't," Emmie said.

"Okay. One of you needs to tell me what's going on. Emmie, you haven't said a single word. I knew something was up the minute you came in," Beth said.

Emmie shrugged her shoulders and didn't say anything.

"I've got to clear Drew's name."

Beth's mouth dropped as she stared at me.

"Why on earth would you do that?"

"Great, none of my friends support me."

"Honey, he left you," Beth said.

"I'm well-aware of what Drew has done. I was there for a lot of it. And for everyone's information, we are divorced. There, I've told everyone who matters now. Are you happy? It's over between us."

I held up my naked left hand and flashed it at them. Beth narrowed her eyes at me and shook her head.

"But I've had two dreams about Drew, and my heart, my instinct, my spirit, my gut, whatever you want to call it, tells me he didn't do it. And to me, clearing his name is the most important thing."

Beth's mouth dropped again.

"The first dream I had I was in the warehouse where I met Jazzy, and in it, I saw two people dump the woman and Drew there."

"Wait a minute," Jazzy said. "The warehouse where Jillian kept us."

"Yes. Why?"

"Well, the center where I volunteer is right around the corner from there. Those old ladies like to 'share,'" Jazzy used air quotes when she said "share." We knew that was a euphemism for gossip.

"Do you think they might know something about the day Drew and Vanessa were found?"

"If it will help you sleep at night, Miss Grace, I'll ask them," she replied.

I hugged her.

"Yes, Jazzy, that would be wonderful. I'm at a dead end. When are you going back over there?"

"I can go today if that's all right with you."

"Absolutely, Jazzy. If you can find out anything that will help Drew, I'd owe you for the rest of my life."

"Oh no, Miss Grace. I love you. I'd do anything to help you, and you seem determined to help him. If the ladies at the center know something, I'll get it out of them."

"Thank you, Jazzy."

"I'll see you ladies later. I can't take any more questions or stares."

"Where are you off to, Grace?" Beth interjected.

"I've got to follow up on my clue. I don't know what kind of wild goose chase I'm on."

"Would you like some company?" Emmie asked. Her eyes darted from me quickly to Beth and Jazzy.

"Hon, we have this place well under control. Just have her back in a couple of hours," Beth said and glared at me.

"Yes, ma'am," I said and laughed.

As soon as we were on the road, Emmie started talking.

"So, what's all this crazy stuff and where are we going?"

"Emmie, do me a favor and watch the road. Make sure we aren't being followed. If you think we are, just let me know."

"Fine. What's going on?"

"Drew sent a letter to my mother's house. There's something I need to find, and I'm not sure exactly what it is. There was a clue in the letter that led me to the shop, and the next clue leads me to Magnolia Cemetery."

"Magnolia Cemetery? Why?"

"The card said 'Chew on this. Let our history be buried.'"

"Well that's not cryptic at all, Grace."

"Actually, it's not – to me. My maternal great-great-, a bunch of greats – grandfather and the same number of greats grandmother are buried in Magnolia. His name was Benjamin Chew and hers was Lucy. They lived in the 19th century. Anyway, I found out more about them through that Walk With the Spirits' tour Historic Augusta does. We went on it a couple of years ago. My mother has the history of our family, and I never really paid attention at family reunions. But she insisted we go to this cemetery tour because one of the reenactors was a relative, and she was playing my grandmother, Lucy Chew."

Emmie had a glassy expression. I could tell my details were boring her.

"Uh huh. What's this got to do with anything?"

"Well, I dragged Drew to it. He was not happy. Magnolia is one of the oldest cemeteries in the city with the first burial dating to 1818. Even though the event was in October, it was warm that day. Fortunately, it was shady in the cemetery. Lots of beautiful old magnolia trees. And the gravestones are really cool."

"You're getting way too excited about a cemetery, Grace, and I still don't see why you are going to drag me there."

"I just think it's cool that one of my ancestors is buried there. There are several family members buried in the plot. Benjamin has a huge tombstone, and it talks about what a sensitive and caring man he was. I mean an actual grave marker with an epitaph."

"Enough already. Are you ever going to get to the point?"

"The point is that whatever the clue is it's at my however many greats grandparents' grave."

"Uh huh."

"Well, think about it. It's a cemetery and a really old and large one at that. It's more than 60 acres. It's like hiding a needle in a haystack. Who is going to search a cemetery? And why would they?"

Emmie paused.

"Well, you've got me on that one. Sounds logical to me."

"Besides, it's only a block from the sheriff's offices. It was close for him. It's the perfect place to hide it. There's no traffic here, and it could basically be hidden in plain sight."

"I'm glad you speak Drew."

"Only a little; otherwise – "

"Grace, don't – "

We drove into the cemetery under the archway. I didn't exactly remember where my ancestors were buried. I knew it was on the northern end, but with 60 acres, it would take a while. We stopped in the caretaker's office and peeked inside to find a man at a desk. I tapped on the door. He looked up and smiled.

"Hi, I'm Jerry Murphy. Can I help you with something?"

"Hi, I'm Grace," I stopped short of saying my last name since it had been in the newspaper a lot. "This is my friend, Emmie."

I wasn't sure what to say. Why would I be in an historic cemetery this close to Christmas? I had to think fast; fortunately, Emmie was faster.

"Mr. Murphy, Grace is doing some genealogy, and I love cool old statues, plus I'm an avid photographer and artist. I was wondering; well, she was wondering about her ancestors, Benjamin and Lucy Chew. They died in the 19th century."

"Yes, I've been to the plot before when they did the Walk With the Spirits tour, but I can't remember where," I interjected.

"Oh, that's easy. I can look it up for you," he said, getting up from behind his desk and walking into one of the other rooms. The caretaker's office was an unusual building. It had a central, octagonal shaped room with portraits of the family who donated the funds for it to be constructed hanging on the walls. The rest of the rooms were like spokes from a central hub. He headed into one of the rooms and went into what looked like a bank vault. He pulled out a giant rolodex from what had to have been the 1950s. I glanced on the shelves of the vault. There were large red ledgers on the shelves. The dates of the burials were listed on the spine.

"Here it is," Mr. Murphy said.

He noticed me staring at the book.

"All of the burials were entered by hand. A lot of this information is online at the city's website. I transcribed those records. Would you like to look inside the book?"

I nodded, and he pulled the book down.

"Benjamin died in September 1858," he said, placing the book on a table. He opened it, and I noticed the names beautifully penned.

"Thank you," I said as I snapped a photo of the ledger.

"The site is near the north wall on First Avenue. You will have to park on Second and walk over to First. There's a path, and the plot is surrounded by a wrought-iron fence. It's on the edge of the road."

"I think I remember the site now. Thank you," I said.

Emmie and I headed back to my car. We drove from the office to the spot he suggested. I hesitated before getting out. I wondered what Drew had hidden for me to find.

"What's wrong, Grace?"

"It's such a beautiful place, but it's a cemetery. I can see why they call it Magnolia Cemetery. I've never seen so many huge magnolias in one place."

"True. I never thought a cemetery would be beautiful. I caught glimpses of magnificent pieces of art here - in a cemetery. Statues of angels and children. Just beautiful. You've piqued my interest. I need to come back and explore this place when I have time to meander. There's so much art here."

I tilted my head and stared at Emmie.

"What? There is, Grace. The stone masons who carved these angels and other pieces were at the top of their craft. They are exquisite."

"Okay, Emmie. We'll have to talk about that later. I wonder what Drew left for me."

I got out of the car and walked up to the dilapidated, wrought-iron fence before timidly stepping into the area. I glanced at Benjamin's grave. It had a huge monument and inscription. There were other graves in the raised plot. I wasn't sure where to look. Also buried there were a couple of their children who died young; their eldest son, also named, Benjamin, died four days after his father. Lucy was 90 when she died. There wasn't anything near the elder Benjamin's massive monument, but I looked at Benjamin Jr.'s; he shared a marker with his brother, Currie, who died at the age of 4. It had two columns. I noticed the remains of a flower arrangement at the base of the marker. It was a faded silk arrangement from Christmas but definitely not this one. It was strange because there were few arrangements in the cemetery. I glanced inside and noticed a plastic sandwich bag. I picked it up. It had a flash drive in it and a folded piece of paper.

I stared at it for a moment. I wondered what was on it. I

could feel Emmie hovering behind me. I sat down on the edge of the plot and opened the bag.

If you want that application to the police academy, I know someone. Despite your excellent sleuthing skills, you won't be able to open these files. They are passcode protected, and only one other person besides me has the code. You'd never guess it. I promise. I pulled out a string of random numbers at the end. It's safer for you not to know what's on this drive. You need to take this to Robert Parnell. He's expecting your call. I know you're asking "Why would Drew want me to take this to a reporter?" Good question. The answer is that this keeps you out of the loop. You can't be connected with this. He will call you an anonymous source. I never found the "smoking gun" I was looking for, but I do have enough information on here to get people to start asking questions. And believe me, Robert will ask a lot of questions to the right people. And you are safe.

He would passcode protect everything. He's behind bars and it's still – "my case, Grace. Thanks for your help, but my case." I did wonder what he was trying to protect me from. Robert Parnell's business card, with his personal cell number written in pen, was also in the bag.

I handed the note to Emmie as I walked around the graveside. He was sending me to the press. Another one of the places I didn't want to go. I'd heard Robert on the radio. I was afraid he'd tear me to shreds. Why him?

"Are you going to call him?"

"I don't have much choice, do I?"

"It doesn't sound like it. I wonder what's on there?"

"Me too, and Drew knew that I'd want to know."

"Should we try breaking into it?"

"Emmie, have you learned hacking from the FBI?"

Emmie laughed and handed the card with the phone number back to me.

"That was not my area, Grace."

"You know me, Emmie, I know spreadsheets and accounting

software and how to do searches on the internet. That's about it."

"Are you going to meet with him alone?"

"No. I don't want to be by myself when I meet him. I need to see how soon he can meet with me though."

I bit my lip and stared at Emmie for a few moments. I took a deep breath.

"Look, if Drew told you to get that information to him, that's all you have to do. You don't have to tell him anything."

"I know, but I bet he knows something else."

"Grace, this could be dangerous. I really do think Drew is trying to protect you, not keep something from you."

"Emma Elizabeth -"

Emmie quickly interrupted me.

"Oh no, you just called me by my full name. What am I in trouble for?"

"Nothing, but you can't tell a soul about this. Especially not Butch. He already thinks I'm plotting against the sheriff's department."

"Sweetie, you have nothing to worry about where Butch is concerned. I already told you that I was planning on breaking up with him anyway. I don't appreciate the way he acted last night, and like I said, he's been erratic. So don't apologize and don't worry."

"Fine but when I say 'no one.' I mean no one. No Beth; no Jazzy no one."

She raised both of her hands.

"I promise. If it makes you feel any better, I'll swear it on your however many greats grandparents' graves."

I laughed at her.

"Fine, I'm doing this to help Drew," I said as I started dialing the number on the card.

I thought it might go to voice mail, but the call was answered after only a few rings.

"Mrs. Ward, I've been expecting your call," the voice on the other end of the line said. It startled me. I certainly didn't expect he'd recognize my number.

I stammered. I didn't know what to say.

"Well since you know who I am, I have some information for you."

"Where are you now?"

"Magnolia Cemetery."

"Can you meet me in North Augusta at the park near the community center?"

"Yes. I can do that."

"Are you coming alone?"

"No, I'll have my friend, Emmie with me."

"Investigator Ward told me she might come with you."

Drew thought of everything, didn't he? On the drive over the Savannah River linking Georgia and South Carolina, Emmie looked up Robert Parnell's photograph at the radio station's website, so we'd know who we were looking for.

Emmie didn't say much on the drive, which was highly unusual for her. This time it was me to break the tension.

"Emmie, you have to say something. This is totally unlike you."

"I was just thinking about all this and wondering what's on this flash drive. You don't need to know what's on here. Whoever did this murdered one person and made it look like Drew did it. This could be really dangerous."

"I know, Emmie, and that's the reason Drew password protected everything. I just wonder why he's trusting Robert."

"Robert has a lot of enemies. There's one politician who Robert repeatedly reported on. Finally, the guy moved to another state, where he tried to run for an office. Things didn't end up well for the politician. Robert's reporting followed him, and people found the same problems – mainly fraud, questionable financial transactions. The guy sued Robert. I've also heard he gets death threats. But on the other hand, I've seen some shady people put behind bars because of his reporting. He won't back down from what he believes. So, people either love him or hate him. If you've done nothing wrong, you don't have anything to be afraid of."

"It's not me I'm worried about. I know it can't be good for Drew. I've seen him in my dreams. He looks like he's been beaten up."

"I know, honey. I know we've given you a hard time about this, but you're doing the right thing. You're standing up for something you believe in, and that's not always an easy thing to do."

"Really?"

"Yes."

I found a place to park and paused. Memories flooded back. Drew and I had been to this park a few times. In the summer, the arts council put on an outdoor concert series, which was a lot of fun. We'd bring a blanket and a picnic basket. Sometimes, he'd dance with me. We loved beach music, and I can shag. We had so much fun. I paused; I could feel the tears again. Was everything going to remind me of him? I guess it would. Always.

"Grace, are you okay?" I heard Emmie ask.

"No, but I will be."

That seemed to be my go-to phrase these days. I was hopeful that one day these wounds might heal.

I didn't see anyone at the park. We walked to the outdoor stage and sat down. I remembered the bands I'd heard – a jazz band, a military band, and then there was the rockabilly band but that concert was moved indoors because of spring rain showers. There were several beach music band concerts we attended over the years. They were always fun. I just wished they lasted more than six Thursdays out of the year.

Within a few minutes, a car pulled up, and its driver looked like the photo we'd seen on the website. I could feel my heart racing a little. I wondered if he would tell me anything that could help Drew. I just wanted to get him out of jail, so I could go on with my life.

"Grace Ward?" he asked without even glancing at Emmie. "You look just like the photo your husband showed me."

"Yes, I guess you're Robert Parnell?"

"Yes ma'am, I am."

I clutched my purse.

"Hi, I'm Emmie. Big fan of your show," she said putting her hand out to shake his.

He smiled.

"Thank you, Emmie. It's nice to meet both of you. I've heard about you, Emmie, and of course, you too, Grace."

"Mr. Parnell,"

"You can call me 'Robert.'"

"I don't want to be interviewed."

"I have strict orders, Mrs. Ward, from your husband. I will never tell anyone about this meeting unless I have your permission. You are a confidential source, and I will not jeopardize that relationship. Second, your husband told me that I was to do everything I could to keep you out of this. I'm sorry about mentioning your name on the radio the other day. But he'd asked me to do that if something happened to him. He said he hoped it would protect you if people knew the two of you were estranged."

"We're more than estranged. Our divorce was final a couple of days ago. Not my choice, but his," I'm not sure why I said that. When I got nervous, God only knew what would come out of my mouth.

I pulled the drive out of my purse, still in its plastic bag.

"What's on this?"

"I'm afraid I can't tell you that, Mrs. Ward. It's another one of Investigator Ward's rules."

Sounded like something Drew would do.

"Will this get my hus – ex-husband out of jail?"

He looked grim.

"I don't think so. It implicates a couple of deputies in some illegal activity, and that's all I can tell you."

"Why would Drew give this to you?"

"Because he was afraid that the evidence might disappear. He suspected one of his superiors but didn't know which one.

Frankly, he wasn't sure who to trust. He was also concerned about the ramifications. He was concerned about both his and your safety. And I'm not worried out that – ramifications, that is or the evidence being 'lost.' I will make sure someone answers the allegations."

"Why didn't he just send it directly to you, Mr. Parnell?"

He laughed.

"It's Robert, and you said didn't want to be interviewed, but you sure are interviewing me."

"I'm sorry. If Drew wanted me safe and wanted this information to go to you, why didn't he just send it to you directly?"

"Maybe he didn't trust me, but now there are two other witnesses to this. You can hold me accountable."

I paused.

"Are Patrick Steed and Mitch Colley involved in this?"

"I can't tell you that although I can tell you that Colley has been caught up in some illegal substance abuse charges in the past, but nothing ever stuck to him. He's got a loud mouth, and I heard about some drugs that went missing after a bust, but nothing was ever linked back to him. And as for Steed, I don't know anything about him. I've never even heard the name before."

"What about Capt. Howard?"

"Are you sure you don't want to go into law enforcement or journalism? You ask a lot of questions. Many of them are good ones. I can't tell you about specific people, but as you know, Investigator Ward came to me because he thought someone higher up was involved."

"Capt. Howard is over him, isn't he?"

"Yes, but there are other higher-ups, not just him so it could be him or several other people."

I thought I might cry again.

"Drew didn't do this. I know he's being set up. Whoever is on this drive is behind it. I know it."

"Ma'am, I believe Drew Ward to be a man of integrity, but the evidence –"

"The evidence was planted. I know it, and I'll bet your gut tells you the same thing. He's a good man even if he chose to end our marriage," I knew I sounded desperate.

"Instincts can be good things, and yes, my instinct tells me something isn't right in all of this. If you can do something to prove he's innocent, I'll do whatever I can to get that information to the right people. You've got my personal cell number, and I promise to answer it. I don't know if you know it, but Drew was arraigned this morning. He pleaded not guilty to voluntary manslaughter. The judge set bond at $250,000."

I hung my head and wanted to cry. I felt Emmie's hand on my shoulder.

"He didn't do it, and where's he going to come up with that kind of money?"

"I have to tell you. It doesn't look good for him."

"No, it doesn't. Please, Mr. Parnell, please do something."

He paused. He seemed to be sympathetic to me, but I wasn't completely sure. My heart ached; $250,000 bond. He was probably going to stay in jail. I hated the thought.

"Are you going to give me the drive?"

I glanced at the bag. It's what Drew would've wanted so I handed it to him.

"Trust me, Mrs. Ward, you don't want to be involved in this any more than you already are. Your husband was concerned about your safety, and he might have reason for that."

"I'd rather have my eyes wide open than be in the dark."

"I understand that, but on this," he held up the flash drive. "It's better for you this way, and I promise you I'm going to get right on this. Thank you. It was nice to meet both of you."

With that, he turned and headed to his car. I sat back down and pulled out my phone. I hadn't had any time to search the internet concerning Patrick Steed and Mitch Colley.

"Grace, what are you doing?"

"Searching for answers. You search for Patrick Steed. I'll take

Mitch Colley."

There were a few references to Mitch Colley, but they only reiterated what Robert Parnell had said. I found some newspaper articles. Some illegal drugs confiscated in a bust by Colley had gone missing from evidence, but nothing was ever linked to him, just as Robert had said. The drugs were never found. He'd also been in a serious car accident a few years ago. He was in intensive care for a while. His brakes had failed going around a sharp curve, and he was flying. There was a photo of the car. It was a miracle anyone got out of it in one piece. He was able to return to duty, and he had no signs from the crash except for a few scars. I passed my phone to Emmie and she passed hers to me.

Her search for Patrick Steed was vague, and nothing stood out at all about the guy. He seemed pretty clean.

"I sent a text to someone at the FBI."

"Can you get in trouble for that?'

"It was just a text. Whether or not anything comes of it is another story."

"We just have more dead ends then?"

"Grace, you may have helped put some crooked cops behind bars. You never know."

"I don't care. When I said I wanted to help Drew, I meant clear his name. I don't care about the rest of this. I want him out of jail."

She put her arm around me.

"It's going to be okay."

"It feels like dead end after dead end, Emmie."

"I know, but something will break through. It always has in every case you've been on in the past."

"Thanks. It just needs to happen soon."

"I know, sweetie, I know."

We sat in the quiet for a few moments. I took a deep breath.

"So, Emmie, what are your plans for the rest of the day?"

"Well, Beth said I only had a few hours, so I guess I should go back to work. Why don't you go back to Trevor's and do more of your internet searches there? The shop has been busy with flower and gift orders."

"I know. I should be there with you. It's my shop."

"Look, throwing yourself into work is great, but don't you need some time to adjust?"

"I've been adjusting just fine."

"No, sweetie, you haven't."

"But it's not up to you to keep the shop running. It's Christmas, and you have families of your own to take care of. I have —" I paused as the tears started to form again. "I have nothing."

She grabbed my hand and squeezed it hard.

"That, sweetie, is where you have it all wrong. You have the potential for something beautiful. And as your best friend, the one who was next to you and held your bouquet when you married Drew at Christmastime 11 years ago, I can't let you screw this one up."

"Like I screwed up the other one?"

"Nope, I didn't say that, Grace, and you know it. I'm no doctor, but you need time to rest. You need a break from your stress. My mother is having a ball with my sons. Don't get me wrong. I love them, but they are a handful sometimes. This has actually been a break for me for a few days. I'm telling you that we don't mind it. Besides, there have been reporters calling the shop for you but not to buy flowers."

"Really?"

"Yes, there have been several. A cop who kills makes news, and they want to talk to people close to him. Don't look now, but your phone is ringing."

Emmie handed me my phone. It was Trevor.

"Hi."

"So, how's the morning?"

I didn't know quite how to answer that one.

"I was wondering if you'd have lunch with me," he said when I didn't respond to his question.

I glanced at Emmie. She was close enough that she could hear the conversation. She nodded at me as though I'd better say 'yes.'"

"I'd love that. I can be there in about 30 minutes. I have to drop Emmie off."

"Ah, your partner in crime-solving. Sounds like you have a story to tell. I'll see you soon."

She stared at me after I ended the call.

"He wants to have lunch with me, and yesterday, he asked me to the Nutcracker tomorrow night in Columbia."

"Sounds like a date, but do you have anything appropriate to wear?"

"Do people still get dressed up for that?"

"In my opinion, they should. Besides, it's Christmas. Christmas is special and so is the ballet. You should wear something sparkly and dressy. Didn't your mother dress you in those red velvet dresses when you were little? You know – for the family Christmas photo."

I laughed.

"Yes, and she made me wear the most obnoxious, gigantic bows in my hair."

"Sounds like my mother. But I bet Beth has a dress you could borrow."

I wrinkled my nose.

"Beth's style is not mine."

Emmie laughed.

"Beth has a great style. It's classy and elegant with a smattering of sexy."

"It's that smattering of sexy that I don't want."

"Grace, you're a beautiful woman, and you aren't dead."

"Thanks, Emmie. I realize that you think Trevor and I should be together. I get that, but I have to get my head together and Drew out of jail before I can move on."

"I'm helping you get ready for this fantastic date."

"Fine, Emmie. Let me take you back to the shop, and I'll get out of your hair."

"Yes, ma'am."

6

Trevor was in the kitchen when I returned. I still felt weird going into his house without knocking, but he insisted I do that despite telling me I was a guest. He smiled.

"I wasn't sure you'd be coming back today."

"Emmie told me that a few reporters had called. I'm not quite up to that so she sent me home."

As we were talking, I noticed a small, white linen-covered table for two, set with the most beautiful china. Trimmed in gold, it had a brilliant poinsettia and holly pattern. The glasses were cut crystal, and the silverware was gold-plated.

"My mother's Christmas china. I thought I'd get some use out of it. She always loved it."

"It's beautiful."

"Cooking is therapeutic. I know I haven't quite accepted the fact that my mother is dead. Touching her dishes this morning hit me hard, so I've prepared a braised beef with rice pilaf, a strawberry, spinach salad with feta cheese and a champagne vinaigrette dressing."

"It smells delicious, but if I stay with you much longer, I'm going to get fat."

I laughed. His eyes twinkled as he smiled at me.

"I've heard about your binges with Emmie, and if those don't do it, you'll never get fat. Besides I've noticed you've lost several pounds since Drew filed for divorce. Pounds you probably didn't need to lose."

I didn't answer that.

"Could I help you put lunch on the table?"

"Still my guest, Grace. Just go sit and let me take care of everything. Since you always insist, you can help with clean-up," he said and winked at me.

I did as I was told. I didn't feel like making decisions. Emmie was right. I was tired. I wanted to relax. And he was still too perfect. Maybe he was OCD and that was the reason he was so nice. He didn't want me getting the kitchen dirty. He wanted everything a certain way. Or maybe he was just perfect – too perfect.

"Why are you staring at me like that, Grace?" he asked as he switched out the Christmas plates on the table with gorgeously plated food.

"Because I still don't think you're real."

"Because I like to watch 24-hour food channels?"

I laughed.

"I guess there's no crime against that."

"I hope not although some of the dishes they've served on some of those challenges are downright criminal. I promise to never serve you one of those or ask you to make one."

He laughed.

"Well, there's no crime in this meal. It's absolutely incredible. You're amazing. Are you thinking about doing something with cooking as a career?"

He shook his head.

"I have several avenues I'm considering, and that's not one of them."

"It's a shame."

"Owning a restaurant is time consuming, and I don't want to live my job. I want cooking to be an enjoyable outlet for me," he said and then paused. "It's amazing how you can deflect every conversation to avoid talking about things."

"I suppose you're waiting for me to tell you about this morning."

"Grace, I want you to be comfortable enough with me to simply talk to me without my having to drag it out of you."

"I do feel like I can tell you anything, but no one wants me to help Drew. And this morning was definitely an adventure."

I told him about the clues and the meeting with Robert Parnell. I wasn't sure what else he wanted to know.

"I'm hoping the information will lead to something, but Robert said it probably wouldn't help Drew get out of jail. I don't know what else to do."

Trevor put down his fork and reached across the table to touch my hand.

"Grace, you're not Drew's savior. You should know that by now."

"I know, but there was just something in his voice. If you'd heard him, you'd know why this is so important. But thank you for everything."

"I haven't done anything."

Throughout the meal, I could hear my phone vibrating on the tiled, kitchen island. It was becoming annoying

"I need to turn my phone off," I said as I got up.

When I picked up the phone, I noticed multiple missed calls from Deputy Steed and Jazzy.

"Do you need to call someone?"

"Maybe. I have calls and one text from Deputy Steed and a couple from Jazzy."

"We were finished eating, weren't we?"

"Yes, but I need to help you clean up."

"I told you I won't fight you on that, Grace."

I was hesitant to call Deputy Steed especially after the way he'd treated me during our conversation. I wasn't sure why he wanted to talk to me. I decided to call Jazzy first because she never called me. Then I remembered her telling me that she was going to go to the senior center. Maybe she had some type of news. I was more interested in getting Drew out of jail than I was in cleaning up the sheriff's department. I didn't care about that one iota.

"Finally, I was tired of getting your voice mail," Jazzy said as she answered.

"Well, hello to you too."

"You need to get down here as soon as you can and bring Dr. Trevor too. A handsome man will go a long way to getting some information from these grandmas. They like handsome men. And they've definitely got some info for you. I've sweet-talked some of it out, but bring in reinforcements. The center is right around the corner from the warehouse Jillian kept us in."

"I know where it is."

Sometimes, I had nightmares about the place. They were all the same. In them, it was a showdown between Drew and Jillian, the woman masterminding the sex trafficking ring that Drew broke up in April. I supposed I had something to do with it, and I wasn't completely sure Jillian was the ringleader. She could've been middle management for all I knew. Not the lowest rung of the ladder but maybe not at the top either. Drew kept telling me I had great instincts, but she duped me. I thought she was innocent in all of it, and it turned out she was behind it. I was so naïve. Drew was so wrong about me.

"Grace," I heard Trevor calling my name. I'd slipped into my thoughts. I wondered how long he had been trying to get my attention.

"I'm sorry. We've been summoned."

He raised an eyebrow.

"Jazzy said there's information that might help Drew, but she said that a handsome man might help extract it."

"And –"

I took a deep breath.

"Jazzy said you're the right handsome man for the job. I'll tell you in the car. It'll save time. We can take mine because I know where we're going."

Once inside the car, I followed through on my thoughts. I hadn't wanted to dwell on those dreams. I tried to dismiss them.

"So, not long after I was drugged and kidnapped, I was thrown into a warehouse where they kept the girls they were trafficking. That's where I met Jazzy."

"Right."

"Well, I thought I might die that day. Jillian's right hand man was an undercover FBI agent. She left me with him; he was supposed to kill me. He'd contacted Drew, and they arrested Jillian. Everything was hunky dory. I don't know when I started having the nightmare, but in the nightmare, I could hear the tapping of Jillian's stilettos against the concrete floor of the warehouse. Then, I can feel the cold steel of the barrel of a gun in my temple. Other things are hazy. I can hear her voice, and I can hear Drew's. It's like I'm not even there. They talk over me. I don't really know how it ends. It scares me, but at the same time, it doesn't. I know that makes no sense."

"How many times have you had this dream?"

"Six, maybe seven times? I've tried not to keep track."

"Why not?"

"Because I don't want to think about it, Trevor."   ."

"Do you believe it's something more?"

"I don't know what I believe. It's hard to describe to people because they can't see inside, and I can't find the words. But there are nighttime dreams, and then there are these types of dreams. And yes, this is as vivid of a dream as any that have come true. But it can't possibly happen. Jillian's in some federal penitentiary somewhere, and Drew is behind bars too. Plus, he's no longer part of my life. I think it's just a coping mechanism or something. Besides, I haven't had the dream since before Drew left me. It's just the whole idea of going down to the senior center which isn't far from the warehouse. I feel like I'm suffocating."

"Do you want me to drive? You can give me directions. I did live here once you know."

"I know. We'll be there soon."

"Why didn't you say something earlier?"

"Because I'd really been trying hard to forget that dream."

I didn't say much the rest of the drive. I concentrated on breathing.

We parked in front of the center and went inside. The building was old, but it was clean. There was one large room where most of the people were gathered. Christmas carols played in the background. The room had several tables in it and a couple of televisions. A couple of men were playing checkers while some of the women sat knitting and talking. As soon as Jazzy saw us, she rushed over. Something was wrong. She seemed scared. She pulled us aside.

"Okay, you're not going to believe this, but you've got to understand these ladies are afraid. That's why I asked you to bring Dr. Trevor. I know he's got a good bedside manner, and he's very calming. Plus, he's easy on the eyes."

She winked at him when she said that.

"Jazzy, slow down. What's going on?"

"You just need to talk to them yourselves, but I know these ladies, they probably won't want to talk to you, Miss Grace. At least not what they need to tell you. I have a feeling they'll talk to him."

Trevor furrowed his brow.

"You'll see," Jazzy said as she led him to the chairs where two elderly women were crocheting. One of them had light pink yarn and the other used light blue.

"Ladies, this is Dr. Trevor Blake. This is Miss Millie and Miss Gertrude. They are making caps for the babies in the NICU at the children's hospital."

"Jazzy, it's Grammy, not Miss Gertrude. Gertrude makes me sound like an old lady," said the woman making the blue cap. She was slender and had perfectly coifed, white hair. Miss Millie was heavier set with shorter hair.

"Gertie, that's because you are an old lady," Millie retorted and then laughed.

"Speak for yourself. Age is a number."

'Whatever. I know I'm an old lady. I feel it in my bones."

"Both of you look lovely today," Trevor said as he sat down. They were near a table but not too close that it impeded their hands. Trevor sat at the table.

I knew why Jazzy wanted him to come with me. He struck up a conversation with them with great ease. You would've thought he'd known them for years. He had the two of them laughing. Jazzy and I didn't exist. Jazzy nodded at me as if to say "What did I tell you?"

Trevor caught my eye once and winked at me. He seemed to be enjoying himself thoroughly.

"Are you any kin to those other Dr. Blakes in town?" Millie asked.

"Yes, ma'am, I am."

"Must've been your father, but he saved my husband's life in the 80s. John had a quadruple bypass, but the old fool wouldn't give up his cigarettes and fried chicken."

"A lethal combination," Trevor said.

"Five years later, he had another heart attack. He didn't make it through that one."

"I'm sorry to hear that, Miss Millie. Have you been to a doctor recently?" he asked.

"No, sir. Not since my doctor died. No one took care of me like he did."

I noticed Trevor was staring at her neck.

"I have three brothers with practices in the area. I don't have an office of my own here, but could I get a closer look at your neck?"

She looked stunned as he moved around to her side of the table.

"What kind of doctor did you say you were?" she narrowed her eyes suspiciously at him.

"I'm an oncologist," he replied.

"Oh, I definitely don't want to go to your office."

He laughed.

"I get that a lot," he said.

"What is it, Doc?" she asked.

"Miss Millie, I have a brother who's a primary care physician, one who's a cardiologist and another who is an obstetrician. I'd really like to see about getting you into see my brother who's the primary care doctor."

"Why, what do you think it is?"

"It could be nothing. He'd need to check it out. Without tests, I wouldn't venture to say."

"That sounds scary, Doc."

"I don't mean to frighten you. What's your last name?"

"Johnson."

He pulled out his phone and made a quick call.

"He can see you on Monday. Do you have a way to get to his office? It's near MCG and University."

She nodded.

"Is he as good looking as you?"

"We have the same genes so he's not bad to look at. You'll like him."

He smiled at her and winked.

I sat back and observed. The two women didn't notice I was there, and that was fine with me. I marveled at him. He was so at ease talking with them. He genuinely cared. He asked them questions about themselves, and they beamed. They even giggled like schoolgirls at different points in the conversation. It was like I was watching him with his mom all over again. I wasn't surprised that he gave his mom his undivided attention, but he'd just met these two ladies. Jazzy had pulled up a chair near me.

I leaned over to her to whisper.

"You knew what you were doing."

"Yes, ma'am," she said. "And that one is a keeper."

I took a breath. She was right. He was.

I'm not sure how long he talked with them. Part of me wanted them to get to the part that Jazzy had called us about, but I let him do what needed to be done. There was no rushing this.

He asked them about their children, but it was when they got to their grandchildren and great-grandchildren that they gushed and smiled. Grammy, as she repeatedly told Trevor to call her, shot a glance at Jazzy, and I noticed Jazzy nodded back at her.

"Well, Dr. Blake, you've been so kind. We may have some information," she said.

"What kind of information?"

I hadn't noticed, but a young man had walked up. At that moment he leaned down and gave Grammy a kiss on the cheek.

"Grammy, I brought it," he said.

He sat down at the table.

"This is my great-grandson, Stephen; he's majoring in film in college in Atlanta. He's on his Christmas break, and Stephen saw something."

"Well, actually, I filmed something," he said.

He showed us his camera.

"I'm playing with some ideas for an independent film, so I wanted to take some shots around town."

He looked terrified and glanced at his grandmother.

"Grammy, this could get you in a lot of trouble."

"I don't understand," Trevor said.

"We're poor people on the wrong side of the tracks," Grammy interjected. "There's one police officer who is on the side of the drug dealers. He makes sure they never get arrested. No one would ever believe us, but you're a doctor. They'd believe you."

Stephen looked around and whispered.

"There are other people with pictures. And there's another angle of this on my phone."

"You filmed with both of them?"

"No, my girlfriend was there too."

"What's on your video?" Trevor asked.

"I was in one of the warehouses. The lighting wasn't all that great. I couldn't believe they did this during the day though. Here."

He handed the camera to Trevor. He played it back. I got closer to look over his shoulder. You couldn't see everything that was going on, but the audio was loud and clear.

"This all has to look like Drew did it," said the voice in the video. "Everything about the crime scene has to look like he killed her. Drag him over here."

I had a sinking feeling. There was an echo. One of the voices sounded familiar, but I couldn't place it right off.

Whoever was talking had a flashlight. He shone it on the ground. I watched as one of the men positioned Drew's body. I couldn't see the man's face. I wondered if he was a deputy. Then, the screen went black for a minute. I heard two gunshots and the body of a woman appeared in the light of the flashlight. Blood pooled around her. I covered my mouth. They just killed her for no reason.

"Put the gun in his hand. Splash some alcohol on his clothes. It will look like he's been here for a few hours; by then his blood alcohol level will have dropped. Tests won't show he's that drunk, but the drugs in his system should keep him out for a while. We can time it so someone comes before they completely wear off."

"Are you sure those drugs won't show up? Everybody knows Drew doesn't use. He might drink, but he doesn't touch drugs."

"We'll have our guy put in a call to 911 soon enough."

I heard laughter. It was chilling. I felt sick to my stomach, but at the same time, I hadn't been this happy in a long time. This would get Drew out of jail. This was what I'd been looking for.

"You said you have photos?" Trevor continued.

"Lots of people in the neighborhood have been taking photos for a while. I can show you some," Grammy said.

Trevor held up his hand.

"One second," he said before he turned to me.

"Grace, would you give me your keys please?"

I was confused, but I handed them over.

"Do you need to make a phone call?"

"Yes, I do."

I walked into a corner of the room. I was trembling.

"Are you okay, Miss Grace?" Jazzy asked softly.

I just hugged her and pulled her close.

"Thank you. This will get Drew out of jail, and then my part is done."

I called Robert Parnell.

"Mrs. Ward, I'm going on air shortly."

"I've got the proof needed to get Drew out of jail. I need your help."

"Can you make it to the studio? I promise I will not put you on air. We can talk between commercial breaks. Come around to the back. I'll have someone let you in."

"Yes."

As I ended the call, I felt Trevor's hand on my arm.

"We need to get out of here," he said. There was an urgency in his voice. "Jazzy, will you be okay? Call me immediately if you need me."

"Yes, sir, I will."

He helped me into the car before going around to the driver's side. I wasn't sure why he was driving, but I wasn't asking. It wasn't long until we were out of the neighborhood and onto a major thoroughfare.

"Grace, are you all right?"

"Why would someone do this to Drew?"

Trevor didn't answer right away. He drove for several minutes, before pulling into a space in a shopping center parking lot, and he turned to look at me.

"Grace."

I was confused especially because Trevor seemed a little shaken. That was out of character for him. He was always calm, even in the darkest times of his mother's illness and death. Knowing he was flustered scared me.

"Grace, in the second recording, you can see the faces better. The lighting is different and so is the angle. While you were on the phone, I watched the second one," he was agitated as he paused momentarily. "Didn't you recognize the voice on the recording?"

"There were two voices."

"Yes, there were, but are you sure you didn't recognize one of them?"

Just then it dawned on me. I wasn't sure why my brain was blocking it out, and I realized why Trevor insisted on driving. I gasped and placed my hand over my mouth. I couldn't believe it.

"Oh my God - That was Butch."

I sat back in my seat and took a deep breath. How could I not have realized? How could Drew not have known? How could Butch have done that?

"Yes, it was. He's involved in some dangerous things, Grace."

"But Butch was Drew's friend. He was Emmie's - Oh no, I'm going to have to tell Emmie."

"Listen, no one knows about this yet. She doesn't know. We'll figure out how to tell her. I know you want to help Drew."

I tried to breathe.

"How could he come to your house the other night, knowing what he'd done? How could he stand in front of the police station and tell me he wanted to protect me for Drew?" I paused again and tried to control my breathing. "No wonder he was so upset when I suggested that it was someone in the department. I can't believe it. All the things he told Emmie I guess those were lies to throw us off. No wonder he wanted to come to dinner. But Emmie is always so good about reading people."

"Well, you did say she wanted to break up with him."

"Yes, Emmie said he'd been different."

"We don't know all the pieces. Maybe Drew was just going to turn him in on the drug deals and for covering the dealers? I don't think Drew suspected Butch would turn on him that way, Grace. He wasn't the one who fired the shots though. He also didn't want Drew killed. He was the one who wanted them just to frame him. His voice seemed shaky."

"Is that supposed to make it better?"

"No, not at all, but it makes me think that he was coerced into this. If that's the case, then Drew didn't think he would be a threat. He certainly didn't think his friend would turn on him this way."

Nausea rose up, and I felt light-headed. I just couldn't believe this.

"Trevor, what do we know? We know Butch didn't act alone. I don't know who else was in that video. We still don't know who the superior was. That's who Drew was afraid of. What other information do you have?"

"There are tons of photos of Butch with people that they said are known drug dealers. I don't know that to be a fact, but there are some unsolved drive-by shootings in that neighborhood."

"Really?"

"Jazzy told me that. We can find out details later. Maybe this is the piece to put the entire puzzle together," he said.

"Do you think anyone would testify?"

"I think it's possible, but they're all afraid. They don't feel anyone has listened to them. Stephen was concerned about his great-grandmother."

"I don't blame them. I just can't believe Butch would do this. He was always so nice."

"What about that other deputy who keeps calling you?"

"How did you know about that?"

He picked up my phone from the center console. It showed a missed call from Patrick Steed.

"Trevor, I don't know who to trust. He seemed nice at first, but then he threatened me, but so did Butch and so did Capt. Howard. Drew trusted Robert Parnell so I have to trust Drew."

"Drew also trusted Butch."

"I know. And I know there's absolutely no way Drew knew that Butch would do something like this."

"There are backup copies of this. But if Robert Parnell is in on this too, you and I could be putting ourselves into danger."

"We have to try, Trevor. Who knows what else they're involved in?"

"All right, Grace."

We drove to the radio station, and I sent a text to Robert when we arrived. Someone opened the back door to the station, and we walked in.

"At the top of the hour, Robert will have about 10 minutes to talk to you for the headlines, weather report, traffic outlook, and sports."

We were left alone in a kitchen area while we waited for him. Trevor had returned to his calm demeanor. I was the one getting more nervous by the moment.

"Mrs. Ward," Robert said as he walked in the room.

"This is my friend, Dr. Trevor Blake."

"Dr. Blake, my condolences on your mother. She was a great supporter of the arts in Augusta and so many other charities. She was a friend of my mother's. I'm sorry I didn't make it to the funeral; I know she will be missed."

"Thank you."

"So, what do you have?"

"We have a video," I said.

"Actually, there are two videos. We've brought one. But how do we know we can trust you?" Trevor said.

Robert raised an eyebrow.

"To be honest, Dr. Blake, you have no way of knowing you can trust me. I can give you my word that things are happening on what Mrs. Ward provided earlier."

"There's so much more."

"And that's the reason your husband wanted to keep you safe."

"Are they looking into Butch Childress?"

"Yes, ma'am. I've been told a formal investigation will be underway shortly."

"He's the one who set up Drew. He needs to be put behind

bars, and Drew needs to be released."

Trevor had Stephen's phone. He pulled up the original video for Robert to watch. Robert seemed stunned.

"A film student took this, and there's a camera with a file similar to this. This has better angles. Just so you know I have a copy of this file in my phone as well. If you don't turn it over, we'll send it to the TV stations."

Robert pursed his lips and shook his head.

"Do you know who else is on the video?" I asked.

"I'm afraid I do, but if you don't, then it's better I leave you in the dark."

"Can you get Drew out of jail?"

Robert held up his phone.

"I'm going to make a call right now."

He walked out of the room. I looked at Trevor.

"I guess we're finished here. I need to go buy some ice cream."

Trevor held my keys out to me.

"No, I think you need to drive. I can't process this. Butch was Drew's friend, Emmie's boyfriend. It's my turn to spend the night at Emmie's. Do you mind stopping at the grocery store, so I can pick up some chocolate chip cookie dough ice cream and then take me to my shop?"

"Absolutely."

I called Beth first.

"Hey, don't let Emmie know you're talking to me. Don't let her listen to the radio or get on social media. And don't let her leave until I get there. Also, keep Jazzy quiet."

"I'll do my best," she said. "Talk to you later."

"How do I tell Emmie this?"

"Well, she did tell you about Drew a few days ago."

The stop at the grocery store was quick. When I got back into the car, Trevor was listening to Robert's radio show

"Investigator Drew Ward was arraigned this morning for the murder of Vanessa Graham. The judge set bond at $250,000. I don't think it's been posted yet, but I hear there's some new evidence in the case that could totally change everything. Stay tuned."

"Maybe we can trust him after all," I breathed a sigh of relief and smiled at Trevor.

"I hope Butch will be behind bars soon, and Drew out soon after," he said.

"You and me both."

It didn't take me long to get the ice cream, and I just let Trevor drop me off.

"I'll be fine. Thank you."

I walked in the back of the shop. Emmie was in the middle of an arrangement when I came in. Beth stared at me, and Jazzy didn't say a word.

"What's going on?" Emmie asked.

"We're going to have a girls' night. I have chocolate chip cookie dough and chocolate peanut butter cup ice cream, plus some extra chocolate chips. Who wants to join Emmie and me?"

"Who died? Both of us are already divorced," Emmie asked sarcastically.

I wondered how to do this. Did I just spit it out? Or did I need to finesse it?

"I wanted to be the one who told you."

"Told me what, Grace?"

I had three sets of eyes staring at me.

"It was Butch."

"What was Butch?" she asked. As the realization hit her, her mouth dropped open, and the shears slipped from her hands.

"He was there when that woman was killed and helped to frame Drew."

"No. It can't be. He and I – "

"I know, Emmie."

"I can't believe I couldn't see through him."

"Do you need me to finish that, Emmie?" Beth interjected.

"Yeah, you'd better, sweetie. Just how much ice cream do you have, Grace?"

"Enough, Emmie."

Emmie grabbed her purse and tossed her keys to me.

"What about the boys?"

"They are staying at your mom's tonight."

She was quiet on the drive to her house. When we walked inside, I took the bag into the kitchen.

"What flavor do you want? Or do you want scoops of both?"

"Just bring me a spoon and the container. I don't need a bowl."

I grabbed a spoon and gave her the ice cream. I put a couple of scoops of the chocolate chip cookie dough in a bowl for me.

"Movies? I think I know your inventory."

"Grace, I slept with him."

I sat down on the couch next to her.

"I'm sorry, Emmie. He was Drew's friend. I thought he was a nice guy."

"I can't believe this," she said, shoveling a heaping spoonful of ice cream into her mouth. "How much of this did you say you bought?"

"Enough. I think," I said. "Although I'm not so sure now."

"I thought I showed bad judgment with my ex-husband, but this sinks to lows I didn't even know existed – I'm done. I'm never dating again – ever," she said, dipping her spoon into my ice cream and mixing it with hers.

"The rest is in the freezer. Do you want it?"

She glared at me.

"I can't believe this. How could I not know I was dating a creep? No, he was worse than a creep. I don't even have a word to describe him. He's evil. I need a shower or to be decontaminated."

"I don't know. Trevor and I were trying to figure out if Drew knew."

"Butch was great at hiding things. Right before Drew was arrested, he started acting very strange. He acted like he was afraid of something or someone. It makes sense now."

"Do I need to escort you to the police station tomorrow?"

"No, I'm not important."

"They still might want to talk to you."

"No. I don't think so."

I sat next to her. I just couldn't eat any ice cream tonight. I was anxious. I kept checking my phone for any updates on Drew's release. I guess those things took time. I didn't know how the legal system worked despite having lived with Drew for so long. Emmie and I watched a bunch of crazy comedies, all of which Emmie cried through. She held my hand.

"I can't believe I ate all of that ice cream."

"Me either," I said. It was approaching midnight.

"You need to get some sleep so you're ready for your hot date with a hunky doctor, tomorrow."

I smiled.

"I don't have anything to wear. I don't even know what I should wear."

"I've seen Trevor's idea of casual and it involves button up shirts and trousers. Does he own jeans at all?"

I laughed.

"Yes, and I've seen him wear them. He also owns sweat pants and even irons them."

"A man who cooks and irons – why haven't you married him yet?"

I laughed again.

"Emmie, I'm really sorry about Butch."

"Don't mention him – like ever again. I have a radar that draws me to bad men or at least bad for me men. My ex-husband's new wife seems to have gotten a better deal. Besides, talking about playing dress up with you is much more fun."

"It's nice to be on the other side of ice cream therapy for once."

"No kidding. I like that side much better. This one is for the birds. So, back to tomorrow. You know Trevor will be dressed in a suit or a tux. You have to be dressed accordingly. Besides, Beth has you covered. We've been talking about this because obviously Trevor bought the flowers from the shop. It was sweet."

"Yes, pink roses."

"And they were all appropriate. Are you nervous?"

"Extremely."

"Why?"

"I just don't know if I'm ready for this. Everything is still so raw, and I just think there must be something wrong with me. Everything is beautiful at first. Remember, I dated Trevor in high school and when he first went to college."

"He was a kid."

"Drew was wonderful too. And then things happen, and they leave. What's wrong with me?"

"Look, Grace, Drew apologized, but he didn't change. Trevor apologized, and if you haven't noticed, he's been trying to show you in subtle and not so subtle ways that he has changed. He's been trying to make it up to you overtime."

She put down her ice cream to give me a hug.

"Nothing is wrong with you except that you try to make everyone happy except yourself. Trevor is an amazing man. You should know that. If he showed any interest in me, I'd be running to the courthouse to get a marriage license."

I laughed.

"Beth has a dress you can borrow, and you are going to knock him out."

She paused.

"Thanks for being my friend, Grace."

"Ditto, friend."

7

I didn't sleep well at Emmie's. I never did. I tossed and turned. If I had any dreams, I didn't recall them when I woke up. I checked the newspaper the next morning. There wasn't anything in it about any arrests. There was a story about Drew's arraignment. "Investigator Arraigned in Slaying" was the headline. I didn't read the story. I was anxious. That meant Butch was still out there somewhere, and Drew was still behind bars.

I sent Robert a text message.

Any idea when there will be any arrests?

I'm being told they are getting warrants, and it should be soon, he responded.

It was a quick response, but it didn't ease my fears any. Butch hadn't tried to contact Emmie. I guess that was somewhat of a relief. And we were going to Columbia later. That gave me a sense of safety.

Trevor had made dinner reservations, and I was starting to get excited about the whole evening. I couldn't remember the last time I'd been excited about anything.

Beth brought several of her dresses to Emmie's on her way to the shop. She laid them out on Emmie's bed for me to choose. We had a couple of weddings to work on.

"Beth, these are beautiful."

Beth touched me on the arm.

"Grace, you deserve some happiness in your life. You've been through a lot, and you definitely didn't deserve what you've gone through."

Three of the dresses were floor length; two were black but one was burgundy. It was off-the-shoulder and had a trumpet flared bottom. It also sparkled slightly. I tried it on first.

Beth smiled.

"That looks better on you than it looks on me," she said.

"I don't think you need to try on any of the others," Emmie said. 'That one is perfect for you. I can't wait to do your hair and makeup. I haven't had this much fun in years."

"I think the last time we did this was for somebody's wedding," Beth added.

"Well we didn't get to do your hair and makeup. You paid to have someone do that," Emmie replied. "My short-marriage came after Grace's, so it had to be mine."

"One thing I like about what we do is that we get to be a part of happy times in people's lives, but I like it best when the happy times are ours," Beth said.

"Hopefully, we'll have a happy celebration with Grace and Trevor," Emmie said. "I'm designing the flowers for that wedding. You don't have much say in it, Grace."

"You are really rushing things. We haven't been on our first date yet."

"Well isn't this it?"

"I guess, but I'm not ready for a relationship yet."

"Stop saying that, Grace. Just let things happen as they should," said Emmie.

"Fine. This will be the dress. Let's go get these wedding flowers finished."

We made quick work of the flowers. That saying about many hands making the work light was no truer than in this moment. And the flowers looked amazing.

Emmie insisted on helping me get dressed while Jazzy and Beth made sure the flowers made it to the weddings. I owed them so much for this past week. They'd never know.

We went back to my house to change.

I stood in the doorway for a few minutes before walking in. I hadn't been in my house much since my divorce was final. It felt different now.

"Grace, are you okay?"

I glanced down at the boarded floor of the porch. I turned to look at the swing before walking inside without answering her question. I took a quick shower before allowing Emmie the opportunity to play dress up.

Beth's dress fit beautifully. I stared at myself in the full-length mirror.

"You are going to knock him out."

"Stop, Emmie. Okay?"

Our moment was interrupted with a knock on the door. Emmie glanced at her watch.

"It's too early for Trevor."

I walked to the front door to see Drew standing there. The sight took my breath away. I threw open the door and hugged him tightly. He'd aged in a short time. He had dark circles under his eyes, and I didn't remember so much gray hair two months ago.

"I'm so glad to see you. How did you get out of jail?"

"Someone posted bond."

I smiled.

"They told me at the shop you were here."

"Come in."

"You look amazing," he said.

"Thank you."

Emmie walked into the room.

"She has a date tonight," Emmie said icily. "With Trevor."

Drew's face fell, and I shot Emmie the most evil look I could manage. She was not happy. She'd folded her arms against her chest and scowled at him, completely ignoring me.

"I'll only take a minute. I just wanted to say 'thank you.' A little birdy told me that you've found some evidence that will clear me of all of this."

"Did you know about Butch?" she asked.

He glanced at Emmie and me.

"All I knew about Butch was that he had taken some money from the wrong people - drug dealers - and now he owed them big time. I didn't know he'd turn on me like he did."

"Has he been arrested yet?" I asked.

"No, there's a process involved, but I imagine it will be soon. Thank you, Grace, for everything."

"Is he the only one?"

"No, one of the investigators in vice was involved plus a couple of people from narcotics. I don't think you know them. There may be one more."

"What about Patrick Steed?"

"He told me he talked to you, and that he's been trying to call you to apologize. You don't answer."

"I didn't know who to trust. And when I talked to him, he sounded like he was threatening me. Besides, you made me a little paranoid."

"I didn't mean to, but maybe that's not such a bad thing."

"Drew, will this clear you?"

"Yeah. It will. I can't tell you how much I appreciate all of this."

I managed a weak smile as Emmie stood there glaring at me. He turned to look at her.

"I'm sorry, Emmie. When I introduced you a couple of years ago, he wasn't mixed up in any of this. When things started getting more serious between the two of you, I was so close to getting enough evidence on him. Then he turned on me."

"What happened that night?" I asked.

"I don't remember much. It all started at his house. He gave me something to drink –"

"It was laced with ketamine."

127

He paused and stared at me.

"Who told you that?"

"It was in a dream, Drew."

He smiled and nodded.

"Of course, it was."

"By the time I woke up, I was in the warehouse and that woman was dead next to me. My bullets in her body."

"Who was she?"

I wanted to know if he was seeing her. Why? I wasn't sure. Here I was getting ready to go on a date with Trevor.

"She was someone who'd asked me for help, and I let her down, just like I let down the two women in this room."

I glanced at Emmie, who'd dropped her arms by now.

"I need to go. I just wanted to thank you again, Grace."

I walked him to the door. He paused before leaving.

"You look beautiful in that dress," he said.

"Thank you."

I watched him as he walked to his car and drove away. I could feel Emmie's stare drilling a hole into my back.

"He's still the same, Grace. He's still the same man who tore your relationship in two because of his drinking problem. You told me you didn't want to see him destroy himself. That hasn't changed."

I turned to look at her. I could feel the tears streaming down my face.

"I know."

She wrapped her arms around me and hugged me.

"I'm sorry, Grace."

After a few minutes, she pulled back.

"You've ruined your makeup," she said as she touched my face. "Come on, let's go fix it. I can't have your puffy eyes ruining my handiwork."

I tried not to think about Drew as she repaired the damage and finished with my hair. She didn't say much either.

Emmie swept my hair back, but she left a few curls. And the

makeup was beautiful. I stared at myself in the mirror. It had been a while since I'd been this dressed up. I felt glamorous.

"You look gorgeous, Grace."

"Thank you, Emmie."

"Try not to cry anymore."

I took a deep breath.

"I can say the same for you."

"I'll bounce back. I always do."

Trevor arrived at 4 on the nose. He picked me up because my car was still at his house. We had reservations for 5:30, and the ballet was at 8.

Emmie was right. He was wearing a tuxedo. The only time I ever saw Drew wear a tux was at our wedding, and the jacket came off before the reception. He smiled as Emmie opened the screen door for him.

"You look absolutely stunning," he said.

"You take good care of her," Emmie admonished him.

"I promise to do that."

He held out his arm for me and walked me to his car. Miss Harper had been a stickler for manners. She was from a different era, and I loved what she'd taught him. Maybe I belonged in a different era too. I was old-fashioned about so many things.

"You always look beautiful, but tonight, you're breathtaking," he said.

The drive to Columbia was quiet. I didn't want to tell him about Drew's visit, mainly because I didn't want to think about Drew. It would start off a chain reaction of tears, and I didn't want to go into the ballet with mascara trailing down my cheeks.

The evening was a fairy tale. Dinner was amazing. It was upscale Southern cooking, and they had shrimp and grits on the menu. So divine. It was probably one of my favorite Southern dishes. Anytime Drew and I went to Charleston or Edisto, we always got them. I wished that everything didn't remind me of him.

"What's the matter?" Trevor asked as I stared at my shrimp

and grits.

"It just reminds me of the last time I had these. Drew had taken me to Edisto. Beth and her husband have a house there. He told me he'd change. I'm sorry."

I tried to smile. I probably should've said something about Drew's visit, but I didn't. I changed the subject instead.

"The shrimp and grits are so delicious. Trevor, do you think you could make this?"

"Absolutely."

The ballet was mesmerizing. They were beautiful and graceful. I had always wished I'd lived up to my name in that aspect. The costumes were lush and had rich colors. At intermission, I got a text from Robert that arrest warrants had been issued for Butch and another name I didn't recognize - a Capt. Jackson. He didn't mention any other names. I did enjoy watching the dancers in the Land of the Sweets, and all of the wonderful Tchaikovsky music that meant so much at this season. It was so much better in person. The colors of the costumes were much richer in person than on the Internet, and we were so close that I felt I could reach out and touch them. The Sugar Plum Fairy took my breath away with her pique circle, and the flowers in the Waltz of the Flowers were breathtaking.

I watched Trevor off and on throughout the ballet. He tried to hide the tears, but I saw him wipe them away a few times. I knew it had nothing to do with the dancing as beautiful as it was. I knew he was missing Miss Harper. I missed her too. She would have loved this. She would've smiled. The second act was her favorite, and she loved the Waltz of the Flowers.

The drive back from Columbia was quiet. Trevor seemed to be lost in thought. I knew watching the Nutcracker was difficult for him. I'd loved that he'd taken me, but I knew he was thinking about his mother. She loved it so much.

About half way into the drive, he broke the silence.

"Did Drew ever take you to things like the ballet?"

"No. He was more of a Saturday afternoon college football

type of guy. I met a professional ballerina back in the spring, and then I found her body. I would've loved to have seen her dance. I know she was even more beautiful than the dancers we saw today. Not that they weren't beautiful, but Alexsandra was amazing. I saw video of her at the memorial service they held for her."

"Mama loved it all. I guess I don't have to tell you that though."

"After we watched all those videos with your mother before she died, I didn't think you'd want to see it live."

"No, but I made Mama a promise to take you since she couldn't go this year," his voice broke. He paused and cleared his throat. "There was nothing more that she wanted than to take you to the Nutcracker like she did when you were younger."

"That's so sweet."

He reached out for my hand and held it. He had such strong but soft hands.

"Your car is at my house, and it's really late. You can stay – in my mother's room if you'd like."

"No, I think I need to go back to my place as tempting as the offer is."

"Are you sure?"

When we arrived back to his house, he opened the car door for me.

"Before you leave, I have something I'd like to give you."

I followed him into the room where his mother had stayed during her illness. That's where all of the holiday decorations were. He walked to one of the Christmas trees, and he pulled out a beautifully wrapped box with a giant silver bow. There hadn't been presents under that tree while she was alive, and I'd never noticed that was there.

He motioned for me to come and sit on the couch in the room. I sat down, but he remained standing.

"Did I tell you how stunning you looked tonight?"

I smiled.

"Yes, several times."

"You've left me speechless. You looked so beautiful tonight."

"Thank you. I had a wonderful time. I know it had to be hard for you."

I wasn't sure where he was, but he wasn't in the room with me. His body was, but his mind was far away. He slowly sat down and stared at the box he held in his hands.

"My mother asked me to give this to you."

He held it out for me to take. I noticed a few tears glistening in the light.

"It will break," he said, holding it until I had a firm grasp on the box.

I sat down, staring at the box. I pulled off the giant bow and opened the box, lifting out a beautiful musical snow globe. It played the Nutcracker Suite and had a view of the home where the party scene was held.

"It's beautiful, Trevor. You didn't have to."

"Yes, I did. That's from Mama. This whole night was her gift to you. As I said, she insisted I take you."

I wiped away a few stray tears. There was an awkward pause. He seemed so sad. I understood now. He was thinking about her final wishes. This had to have been difficult for him. Again, I noticed the tears in his eyes. He hadn't cried much during the funeral or in the past few days. I was wondering if he was just going through the denial phase. He tried to be so strong for everyone else.

"Thank you, Grace, for all you did for my mother," he said.

"I should go now."

"Thanks, I need to be alone for a little while," he said.

He walked me back outside to my car.

"Call me when you get home," he said.

"I will."

I drove slowly back to my house. I really didn't want to go there, but there was no reason for me to stay with Trevor. I got home and made sure I locked all the doors. I took the snow globe and put it on my coffee table. It was the only Christmas decoration in the whole house.

As I started to call Trevor, I noticed a text from Emmie.

How was it? Or am I interrupting something?

Not interrupting anything. Will call in a sec.

I sent a text to Trevor to let him know I was home. I didn't want to call in case he'd already gone to sleep. Only seconds after I hit send, my phone rang. It was Trevor.

"That was a text not a call," he said and laughed.

"I know. You looked so tired. I didn't want to disturb you."

"Not until I know you're safe."

"I am. Good night, Trevor."

I put on some yoga pants and a T-shirt and sat on the couch. I wished I was sitting on his balcony. It felt safer than mine after 1 a.m. I called Emmie.

"So, tell me all about your date."

"Not much to tell."

"You aren't going to give me the juicy details?"

"There are no juicy details to give, Emmie. It was a wonderful night, but it got to Trevor. His mother loved 'The Nutcracker,' and we'd already watched more than a dozen videos of it since Thanksgiving. He was in tears. He went to bed. He said he needed to be alone, and I came home."

"Fine but keep your options open."

"I am. Not to change the subject but has there been any news about anyone being arrested?"

"No, I haven't heard a peep. Just hang in there. I'm sure it's happening. I'll sleep better when Butch is off the street. I still can't believe – oh never mind. I'm going to try to go to sleep. I'll probably cry a little bit more. Call me if you need me, Grace."

"I will. Go to sleep, Emmie."

8

I curled up on the couch. It didn't take long to fall asleep, but my sweet dreams were interrupted a few hours later as I felt cold steel pressed hard against my temple.

"Get up, and don't make a sound," whispered a cold, angry voice.

It was Butch. He reeked of cigarette smoke and alcohol. He had sat down on the couch next to me and leaned in. How did he get in without me hearing him? I could feel my heart pounding in my chest. My brain was all over the place. Questions flooded my mind. Butch had tried to ruin Drew, who I thought was his friend. Did Butch kill the woman, Vanessa Graham? If he had was he capable of killing me too? I swallowed hard and slowly took a breath in. I felt steel clasp around my wrists. My dreams had always been super realistic, but I was sure this was no dream.

"I'm taking you with me."

I sat up slowly.

"Why are you doing this?"

"Don't talk, Grace," he growled.

As soon as my feet hit the floor, the barrel of the gun became wedged into my back. I was glad I'd fallen asleep in something warm. I didn't think I was going to get the chance to put on any shoes.

Before he opened the door, he put his hand over my mouth and pulled me back to him.

"Don't say a single word, or make a sound," he said into my ear.

I walked down my porch step, trying to hold in the tears. I wasn't ready to die.

Butch kept the gun firmly in my back. I was afraid of what he might do. It was still pitch-black outside. I had no idea what time it actually was, but there were no cars on the road. He'd parked on a side street across from the house. With every step, I could feel the gun. The road was rough and hurt my bare feet.

I wondered what I was supposed to be thinking right now. I wondered what I was supposed to be feeling. I prayed under my breath. I didn't think my time was up, but I guess that wasn't for me to know.

The car we got into wasn't his. It was a dark colored, beat up, late model car. I don't think it had Georgia plates on it. It wasn't really suspicious looking.

He pushed me into the car.

"If you try to run, I'll chase you down, and I'll kill you."

I sat motionless as he got into the driver's side and started the engine.

"You just couldn't keep your nose out of it, could you?"

I didn't know what he wanted me to say.

"I thought Drew was your friend. How can you do this? Do you really think that you're going to get away with this? You just kidnapped me."

"Grace, you wouldn't understand, but I'm in over my head. It started out small. I took a cut from a couple of drug dealers and in return, they got away. It was supposed to be a one-time thing, but they had recorded it all. I was in their pocket. It has spiraled out of control. I don't want to do this, but it comes down to you or me. I've done things I can't escape from while I'm here, but you're my ticket out. When I turn you in, I'll walk away with a tidy sum of money. I've got a fake passport, and there's a boat waiting on me at Hilton Head. I'm going to see the world. I wanted to take Emmie with me.

You came between the two of us, and I'll never forgive you for that."

That was chilling.

"Turn me in?"

"All I know is that I'm supposed to take you to the warehouse. What happens after that I don't know, but like I said you're my ticket to freedom. Someone wants me to take you there. They've got arrest warrants out for me. They've already taken in Capt. Jackson. He's the one who's in bed with whoever I'm taking you to. I have no idea. But this ends for both of us when you're delivered."

We kept driving. I didn't want to say much. I didn't want to agitate him. I didn't understand at all. He was Drew's friend. He was Emmie's ex-boyfriend. How could we not know who and what he really was? And I wasn't sure what scared me more – the fact that he was driving drunk or the fact that he had a gun and wasn't afraid to use it on me.

I felt the tears streaming down my cheeks.

"What about Drew? I thought you were his friend – our friend."

"You're his ex. Why should he care what happens to you? And I really liked Emmie, but she sealed your fate when she chose you over me. No one does that."

That stung, and I kept quiet.

We passed through downtown Augusta and into the area near the railroad tracks and some of the warehouses. I remembered these warehouses. They were where the girls, who were being trafficked, were kept during the golf tournament in April. They were where I met Jazzy for the first time. They were where Drew vowed he'd change. My brain was going in so many different directions at one time. And then I remembered the dream that had been haunting me; the dream of Jillian and Drew. Jillian was in a prison out of state last I heard.

We pulled up in front of the warehouse, and he turned to look at me.

"Well this is where I leave, and you stay."

He opened the door and pointed the gun for me to get out. I stood, and he grabbed my arm. The ground was gravel. I thought the asphalt was uncomfortable, but this was sharp, rough, and cold. I had nightmares about these warehouses. I felt my chest constricting. I couldn't breathe. I thought I'd die here in April. Was I going to die here in December instead? There was a street light flooding the outside of the building. He came up behind me and pressed the gun back into my back. He pushed me toward the steps.

He unlocked the door, took off the handcuffs, and pushed me inside. It was the exact same warehouse. It hadn't changed any in eight months. I knew there was no way to get out of this place. I'd tried the last time I was here. He pushed me inside without saying another word, and the door closed with a thud.

I just sat there for a few minutes. The weather finally started to feel like it wanted to be winter, and I was cold. My thoughts were all over the place. We usually had winter in Augusta around January or possibly February. It usually lasted two or three weeks. Not too many freezing temperatures, and ice and snow? What was that? I'd often wondered how many people actually got snow at Christmas. That was anomaly I'd never see. It was 90 degrees at Christmas a couple of years ago. I remember wearing shorts after we'd had the formal dinner with my parents on Christmas day. Christmas Day – what would happen on Christmas Day? It was still about a week away. I pulled my legs into my chest and buried my face in my knees. I continued to pray desperately.

I wasn't sure how long I sat on the floor. I had plenty of time to think of what I'd do if I made it out of this alive. Drew didn't want me in his life, but Trevor did. I'd helped Drew. He was a free man. The charges would be dropped. I could close that chapter, no - that volume of my life. It was over; there was no turning back. Even if – I had to stop thinking that. There was no 'even if' when it came to Drew. I'd begged Drew to get help for his addiction. There, I'd finally come to grips with it. He was addicted to alcohol. It had priority over me and our relationship. It came between us. He'd made promises to change; to get help; but he didn't. He could say he loved me all he wanted, but actions speak louder than words. And is actions spoke, the same as Trevor's actions had spoken. But it had only been a few months with Trevor. Would it stay the same? Would he love me the same in a few months, in a few years, if I got out of here. Rays of light began to seep in through the slats high above. The room was littered; there were broken bottles on the floor.

Now, I could see the blood stains on the floor, where they'd senselessly and callously shot Vanessa Graham in hopes of framing Drew. I walked over to the spot and stared. I wanted to cry over this young woman.

I heard the sound of a key going into a lock. I took a deep breath. I wondered who wanted me as payment.

"Well, look what the cat dragged in," it was Jillian, wearing those stilettos.

I just stared at her. The one dream I didn't want to come true and here it was playing out in front of me.

"Cat got your tongue?"

"I thought you were in jail."

She laughed.

"It's amazing what kinds of favors you can call in," she said. "A few people are still in jail, but they don't have the assets I do. I know some powerful people, honey, and you messed with the wrong woman."

She walked over to me and stared me up and down.

"You know despite your age, you could be profitable, except that you can't have children. I could probably sell you to someone, but childbearing would be part of the deal, and that would negate it all."

I still didn't answer. I tried not to flinch, but she'd hit a sore spot with me. Then she hit me across the cheek, but not with her hand. It stung, and I winced. I heard her laughing. I looked up to see a gun in her hand. I didn't want her to see fear in my eyes.

"What do you want, Jillian?"

"Well, I can't make up for the business I lost eight months ago and ever since. I'm still trying to smooth things over on that. It's been difficult from my jail cell, but not completely impossible. I'll be back up and running pretty soon, or at least as soon as I tie up a loose end. Since our FBI agent friend helped you the last time, I guess I'm going to have to do the dirty work myself."

I stared at her.

"Go ahead."

"That's no fun. You're supposed to at least put up a little bit of a fight."

"Why? You're just going to kill me anyway. So, shoot me."

Somehow though I didn't think she was going to kill me. Although I thought Butch might, I knew Jillian wouldn't. My dream told me that Drew was involved in this showdown.

"Well, just humor me a little. Maybe we could have a catfight."

"You seem to be preoccupied with cats."

She smiled.

"No, actually just stalling because by now, the nosy neighbor who lives across the street and is a friend of Jazzy's has called her. Actually, I sent Jazzy a message too, to expedite things you know. Yeah, I'm still a little angry about you taking a piece of my property and giving her a job, trying to help her better her life or whatever you call yourself doing. I gave her food and shelter, and Jazzy brought in a lot of money. I'm really not sure your deal is better. She was good at what she did until she got mouthy. She had a good thing going, and you took her away. I'm sure she doesn't rake in the dollars for you like she did for me."

I'd never wanted to kill anyone, but about now, I wished I'd had my gun. Jillian was evil. Anyone who saw people as commerce was evil to me. I couldn't understand this.

"Anyway, I expect your knight in shining armor to arrive soon. He's been sprung from jail, so he should have no problem getting here. I know he'll be leading the brigade. I wouldn't want to miss this. I think it will be fun," she smirked. "Let's play this game, shall we?"

I swallowed.

"You're a sick woman."

She laughed.

"See, I have a few friends in the police department. They are going to come in and kill both you and your knight – whichever one decides to come. You do get around, Mrs. Ward. I understand there's another knight in the wings," she sneered as she said "Mrs."

"You think you're going to walk away from this?"

"Of course, I am, silly girl. I have friends in high places. Really high places."

"Who was the woman you had killed?"

"Vanessa? She was one of my girls, but she had the nerve to call Drew for help. I couldn't have another one jumping ship. I still had some business assets while I was behind bars, you know."

Of course, Drew was trying to save her. I wanted to believe that Drew would show up and save me. If one part of my dream had come true, maybe the rest would. I just never saw how it ended. It was morning by now. I could see the light streaming when Jillian came inside.

"He should be here any second now. He is taking forever. Men, you just can't trust them to be on time. And this chit chat is boring me."

As if on cue, Drew burst through the door.

"Don't move, Jillian," he commanded

"It's a trap, Drew," I yelled, and in one quick motion, Jillian was behind me with a gun pointed at my head. She cackled as the metal pressed into my temple.

"Jillian, put the gun down," he said as he trained his gun on her. She was right. She'd planned it all out, kidnapped me, and led him straight to us for her showdown.

"Ah, Detective Ward, it took you long enough to get here, but I'm so happy that you decided to join our little get together. Too bad, your wifey, or should I say ex-wifey didn't make flowers. It would've been a nice touch. Cleared of your charges and back in the line of duty. That was quick. I'm not sure how you pulled that one off. Oh, and it was so sweet of you to divorce your wife for me. You didn't have to do that. You're not really my type – a little old for me," Jillian's voice had turned sing-songy. It was surreal.

"Jillian, put the gun down."

"Oh, you didn't tell her, did you?"

I closed my eyes. I could feel the tears flowing again. She leaned in and whispered in my ear.

"See, Grace, I wrote your husband – I mean ex-husband – a few letters from jail. He has dreamy eyes, and I have this older man fantasy sometimes. It comes and goes."

It was almost like listening to two people. One minute she was sugary-sweet and then the next the voice was low-pitched and frightening. Her voice began to drop.

"I told him I'd hunt him down and destroy everything he loved. So, do you know what he did? He divorced you to keep you safe, but I didn't buy the whole routine about him not loving you anymore. No, I knew that wasn't true. I have so many photographs of you two together. I just hate happy endings. And you'll never get one."

By the time she'd finished her tirade, her voice had dropped to a low growl.

I stared at him. He nodded at me. Although she'd been talking in my ear, he could hear her. There were no sound barriers in the room, and everything carried.

"Oh, I was right. You did divorce her for me," her voice again was sugary sweet. "That makes me so happy, Drew, but I like my older men to be handsome and rich. You certainly are sexy, Drew. Those eyes are to die for. But you don't do it for me on the rich part. So see, you divorced her for nothing."

I felt sick. Now I really did want to kill this woman.

"Come on, Jillian, you got want you wanted. Now, put the

gun down," he tried to talk her down.

"Hmm, I'd have to say 'no' to that one. Right now, I'm using your wife as a shield," she dropped her voice to a deeper tone. She became more serious. "This is the showdown that should've happened in April. You coming to her rescue, but me holding the gun. I shouldn't have let a man do a woman's job. Men, they just let you down. Isn't that right, honey?"

She jabbed me in the ribs as she said that.

"What do you want, Jillian? How can I get you to let Grace go?"

"I want you to try and shoot me and hit her instead, and then your life will be a living hell. Or I'll kill her in front of you when I get done torturing the both of you. I'm enjoying this," she laughed.

I drew another deep breath.

"Gracie, what have I told you?'

"Stop coaching her, Drew. She's got a concealed permit, but she's a pretty easy mark. She's pretty stupid. I bet she really doesn't even know how to use her gun."

She started to laugh. By now, I'd had enough. This woman had ruined my life. I wasn't thinking when my body took over and what Drew had taught me came into play. We'd practiced it so many times in the living room. I'd flipped him on his back numerous times. How had I forgotten? Maybe this was muscle memory kicking in?

She'd let her guard down when she started mocking me. An elbow to the throat and my knee to hers, and she lost her balance. She let go of me to catch herself on those towering stilettos she liked to wear. When she did, I heard a shot or two ring out. I wasn't sure how many. My ears were ringing as I looked on the floor behind me to see her lying face up with her eyes wide open. Blood poured out of her chest. I guess the bullet went straight through her heart. I dropped to my knees on the floor and covered my face with my hands. I would never stop crying.

I felt a pair of arms wrap around me. I closed my eyes. I never thought he'd hold me again.

"See, you remembered what I taught you," Drew whispered into my ear. He pulled me close and rocked me while I cried. I wanted to remember how this felt.

"Where's Butch?"

"Butch's sorry self is in jail. If they would've allowed it, I would've put the cuffs on him myself. But I'm only out on bond. I had to watch him get arrested. I watched them put him in the back of a squad car while we tried to figure out what happened to you."

"I'm so glad to hear that."

"I'm so sorry, Grace. If I'd known this was going to happen, I would've done so many things differently. I didn't know Butch was working with Jillian until it was too late. He had a change of heart as he was being arrested. He told me who had you," he said softly. "I can't ask you to forgive me, but I truly never meant to put you in harm's way. I knew Butch was mixed up in some things. I knew he had drug connections and that he made evidence disappear. I didn't know that he was mixed up with Jillian. Please, Grace, please know that."

I pulled back and looked up at him.

"Of course, I forgive you. You should know me by now. I can't hold onto anger and hatred. That's where it leads," I said gesturing to the dead body on the ground.

"Are you okay?" he asked as he touched my cheek. I winced and drew back. "Did Butch do that?"

"Jillian, I think she hit me with the butt of her gun."

"That's going to bruise. Anything else?"

"I can't think of anything."

"Can you feel your feet?"

I wondered why he asked, but I didn't have on any shoes. I glanced down to see they were dirty and bloody. Just then the realization hit me.

"Yes, and they hurt."

"We'll get an ambulance."

"I'm not going to a hospital."

"Just let a paramedic check you out. Please."

"Wait a minute. You just shot her. You aren't supposed to have a gun. You're out on bond. They'll put you back in jail."

"I don't care. You're alive; that's the only thing that matters to me."

Drew hadn't come to the warehouse alone. Capt. Howard was there, and Deputy Steed, plus several other deputies. I hadn't noticed until now. I'd been so focused on the two of them. I wasn't aware of anything else.

"No, Mrs. Ward, there won't be any charges. Evidence has been presented to the judge to get Drew's case thrown out, and we had several witnesses to this. He acted in self-defense, and I'll testify to that myself," Capt. Howard said.

Drew stood up, and I followed his lead.

"You taught her well, Drew," Capt. Howard said. "She didn't flinch during any of my questions. And she was right about you. But I knew she was. I never believed you could kill someone in cold blood. The crime scene was staged too perfectly."

He reached out and shook my hand.

"More details will come out in the next few days, but this is bigger than you know, Mrs. Ward. Thank you for everything you did."

"Mrs. Ward." The words hit me in the chest. I turned away, so Drew couldn't see my expression. I heard Drew say a few other things to Capt. Howard.

"Who else did you arrest?" Drew asked.

"We'll get you cleared for duty as soon as possible. Come in tomorrow, and we'll talk. This rooted out some bad apples."

Capt. Howard walked away.

"You told them I helped, Drew?"

"I did. But this also sealed the deal. People will say you can alter video, but this we all saw with our own eyes. If I'd known Butch was working with Jillian, I never would've asked for your help."

"I believe you."

"Listen, I need you to" - he started to say.

"Give a statement. I know the drill, Drew."

Deputy Steed took over the questioning.

"Hi, Mrs. Ward. I tried to call you to apologize. I think I sounded pretty harsh when I talked to you."

"I thought you were threatening me."

"No, ma'am. I'm sorry for that."

"I'm sorry I didn't completely trust your motives."

"Not a problem. I understand."

From there, I went into the events of the night and slid into that familiar black hole of numbness. I had so many questions I wanted to ask Drew, but they'd have to wait. This was getting to be old hat – the numbness, the feeling like I was in a cave, the hearing my words come out of my mouth but having no idea what I was actually saying. I wasn't sure how long I answered questions or what they even asked me. I just wanted to get out of this place. I didn't care where I went.

After I gave my statement, I sat on the floor. Someone had brought me a blanket. There were paramedics on the scene. They tended to the place where Jillian had hit me. It stung, but it would be okay. My feet were bleeding from stepping on glass outside the warehouse, and God only knew what else. They cleaned them and found a pair of socks for me. And I think that was a tetanus shot. Ow. I watched Drew. He was talking to deputies. I'm sure they had plenty of questions for him.

"Are you ready to go home?" he asked me once they'd finished.

Home. Did I have a home? I shook my head.

"No, I don't have a home."

My voice was breathy.

"Where do you want me to take you?"

"Nowhere. Drew. I don't want to go anywhere. I don't want you to take me anywhere. Just leave me alone."

"Well, I can't leave you here, Grace. You have no shoes; no

ID, no money with you; no way to get anywhere and no way to call anyone. Do you even have a key to get into the house?"

"No because I think Butch got in using our spare we had hidden in the flower pot."

He picked me up.

"What are you doing?"

"I still can deadlift twice, almost three times your body weight, Grace, and I haven't been able to lift for a few days."

I laughed. He put me in the car and drove me to our house. Our house. He pulled a key out of his pocket. I couldn't go in there. I realized what the date was. Not today. Today of all days. What should have been our 11th anniversary. My chest constricted again. I wasn't sure I could breathe. I wanted this pain to just leave.

"How long have you had that?"

"I hoped things might turn out differently, Grace."

When we got out of the car, he picked me up and carried me into the house.

"I can walk."

"I want to make sure you are okay."

The house was depressingly undecorated for Christmas except for my snow globe. I usually went all out. His concern unnerved me. It opened up another set of old wounds. He gently placed me on the couch.

"Are you hungry?" he asked.

"No. Was she telling me the truth? You left me because of her."

He nodded and sat down next to me. I turned to face him, and he moved in close to me. I stared at him, waiting for his answer. The man who brought me home and sat in front of me now was the man I'd fallen in love with. Kind, gentle, caring. What had happened to him? He gently touched my other cheek.

"Everything I did, I did to protect you. Jillian wrote me. There were veiled threats in them. I'd been holding onto those letters just in case. I knew that Jillian wasn't working alone. I knew there was more to that human-trafficking ring, but I thought that if I made it look like I wasn't in love with you anymore, that we were not living together, that we were done then they wouldn't go after you. From all the evidence I had, Butch wasn't directly involved with her, but his superiors were. It all tied together – the drugs, the prostitution, a lengthy money trail. And I couldn't connect all those dots before they framed me for Vanessa's death."

"Butch told me he didn't know Jillian."

"He didn't; there were several people between him and her, but he'd taken favors from the wrong people."

"Is that what was in the evidence I took to Robert Parnell?"

"Some. There were photographs and documents. I found receipts at his place and uncovered a bank account that had more than I've ever made in it. I overheard a few phone calls when I was supposed to be asleep. But it pushed his hand and I put you in danger. I had been keeping tabs on Jillian, but I've been out of pocket the past few days. No one else knew I was doing that. I never wanted to hurt you. I've made such a mess of everything."

The tears were flowing down my cheeks, but now, they were mixed with sorrow. My heart was torn.

"But that's behind us now. If that's the only reason you filed for divorce, we can start over. You're my husband."

He shook his head.

"Ex-husband, Grace," Drew said deliberately. "Ex-husband. Not that I ever wanted to be that, but I'm still the same man I was before I left you. I'm not the same man I was 14 months ago or 14 years ago when I saw you at that fender bender."

He paused and stared into my eyes.

"Grace, I'm still an alcoholic. As soon as I got out of jail, I started drinking again. That's the reality. That's why you walked out on me in April. Remember? You couldn't take it then. I can't un-see Mark killing Linda. I can't get over thinking I'm the reason she's dead. That Drew would still hurt you. I won't put you through that again. I will never allow you to be kidnapped and your life threatened again.

That's why this has to be over."

"But you can still get help."

"You aren't listening to me. I promised you twice I'd get help, and I didn't. That makes me a liar. I've never been a liar, and I won't lie again. You told me several times that you didn't want to watch me destroy myself, and that you weren't going to. You can't love me through this. Not that you aren't good enough, I'm not good enough. Your love for me won't fix me. I have to fix me. We weren't working – you and I. We didn't work for a long time. I put you through a living hell in the past year. Do you want to keep living there? I'm going to start over somewhere with the realization that I destroyed the best thing that I ever had," he said, choking back the tears.

I didn't want this to be goodbye, but he wasn't changing his mind.

"Grace, let me ask you a question," he paused and seemed to be lost in thought for a few moments. "What's going on with you and Trevor?"

"Nothing. He's my friend. I'm not ready for anything else. He's never even kissed me."

"Why? We're not married anymore. I know you're in love with him. There was something about the way you looked at him even before we filed for divorce, and I saw it."

"I don't know for sure. I have feelings, but I don't know what they are. I'm so confused."

"You should have a life with him. Don't dwell in the past."

I was sobbing by this point. He pulled me close to his chest and kissed the top of my head.

"Trevor should be doing this, not me, Grace," he whispered.

"I still love you, Drew."

He let me go. There were tears in his eyes.

"You love what we had, not what we have. You and I - ," he glanced away. "You love the memory, and memories are always more romantic than the reality."

"Please don't let this be over."

"Grace, is that what you really want?" he paused. "Think about it, Grace. Is that what you really want? Do you want me to stay here with you and you watch me struggle with the drinking problem we both know I have? Or do you want the newlyweds? The ones who laughed about everything. The ones who loved each other like there was no tomorrow."

"Why can't we be that again?"

He smiled and touched my face.

"That's one of the things I've always admired about you, Grace. You have such an innocence despite everything you've gone through. I don't think we can go back to the Grace and Drew who were pre-Mark and Linda, pre-lost babies, pre-murder investigations, pre-death threats. Or at least, I can't go back to that Drew. I almost watched you die twice, and it kills me inside. Without me in your life, that threat is gone. I don't have to worry about someone trying to kill you because they are trying to hurt me."

I hung my head.

"Please, Grace. I don't want to hurt you anymore. That's all I'm good at doing."

He tilted my head back so that I could look into his eyes. He searched my face for the longest time. It was as if he was trying to lock it into his memory. I reached up to touch his cheek, and he leaned over and kissed me. I felt like I did on the night I was so desperate to keep him from leaving. I wrapped my arms around his neck, and he pulled me close to him. There was still something there. Love, passion, lust, I don't know what to call it. I closed my eyes to savor the moment. I felt like I was home now. He was still home to me. But I also knew he was right as he kissed me. Things could never be the way they needed to be if he didn't want to change. He pushed me back and stood up.

"I'm sorry, Grace I shouldn't have done that. I should go."

"Where?"

"Does it matter? If I stay, things will get complicated really fast especially since today is – "

"Yes, today. Today of all days," I raised my voice. Anger had stepped in. I pushed him in the chest. I probably could've hit him, but I didn't. "Eleven years ago today, you promised me; you promised me – forever."

I sank to the floor and wept. He sat on the floor next to me and pulled me into his arms. He rocked me for several minutes as I sobbed against his chest.

"There's nothing I'd rather do with you today than stay with you," he whispered. "But – "

"I don't care, Drew. I want you to stay. I need you to - "

He looked at me and touched my cheek. He had tears in his eyes.

"You say that now, but you wouldn't say it tomorrow when I was gone," he still spoke in whispers. "You'd hate both of us, and you know it. I don't want to make you cry anymore."

He gently pushed me away.

"I need to leave now. Thank you for everything you did to help me and to help solve yet another of my cases, and thank you for saving my life," he said softly.

I looked down.

"I have that application for the police academy if you're ever interested," he said, trying to change the mood in the room.

"No, that's okay."

"Goodbye, Grace."

I sat on the floor and watched him leave. I heard the engine start and the sound of his car as it faded in the distance. I began sobbing yet again. After several minutes, I got up and locked all the bolts on the door. I went into my bedroom where I bolted that one too. I made sure the windows were locked. Then I hid myself in the bathroom. I turned on the hot water and stripped before getting into the water. And then, I cried as many tears as I possibly could. I wanted to cry them all out until there were none left to cry. I cried until the scalding hot water was cold.

By the time I got out of the bath, I heard pounding on my

door, and Trevor calling out my name. I put on a pair of sweatpants and a T-shirt and went out. I didn't want him here. I didn't want him to see me like this. Plus, I felt so embarrassed by what had just happened between Drew and me even though he hadn't witnessed it.

When I opened the door, he rushed in and pulled me close to him.

"I've never been so scared in my life," he said as he buried his face into my hair. "I didn't know where you were. I've been calling you all day. Finally, Jazzy said one of the ladies who goes to the senior center she volunteers at called her about something suspicious at the warehouse. And then Drew showed up at my house. He told me what happened."

Trevor rattled off his sentences in rapid fire. I could tell he was shaken. He never talked that fast. He was always deliberate and methodical in his words. And he was always even-keeled.

I broke free of his embrace and stepped back to look at him.

"Drew came to see you. Why?"

"It surprised me too."

"How long have you been outside?"

"Twenty minutes. I was ready to break a window."

"I need to be alone. Thank you for checking on me," I could hear the ice in my voice.

He looked as though I'd punched him in the stomach.

"Are you okay?"

"No, but I want - I need to be alone."

He stepped back.

"Please leave."

That came out sharper than I'd wanted. He furrowed his brow.

"Grace, I don't want to leave you this way. Do you at least want to talk about what happened? He told me you didn't need to be alone."

"Then you know everything there is to know. He was there for the important parts, so I'm sure he told you what happened. I just want to be alone."

And that came out even sharper. He glanced at the floor and took a deep breath. I'd hurt him, and I didn't mean to.

"You know where to find me," he snapped back and left.

I didn't blame him for snapping. That's all I'd done since he walked in.

I sat in my overstuffed chair and cried; so much for getting all the tears out. Why didn't I tell him? Why did I push him away? I sounded so angry. I guess I was. I almost got killed yet again. I had a gun pointed at my head. And I wanted someone to die. I've never wanted anyone to die. My actions led to a woman's death. Drew shot her because of me. I wasn't sure how I felt about that. And to find out my husband divorced me to protect me from a crazed woman, that he still loves me, but he doesn't want to have anything to do with me made no sense to me. I still didn't understand. Maybe it would've been better if she'd just shot me when she had the chance. I curled up on the chair and spent the next few days in that spot except to go to the bathroom. Everything was a blur. I didn't want to leave the house. Trevor texted several times to check on me; Drew even texted me multiple times to see how I was. That one surprised me somewhat. He'd been so good at keeping his distance, but he broke the silence. I'd never seen anyone killed before despite the fact that dead bodies showing up were becoming a habit. And of course, Emmie, Jazzy, Beth, my mother and brother all texted. My response to everyone was that I was fine, and I just wanted to be alone. I finally let the battery run out and didn't put it on the charger. I counted every crack in the plaster; I knew the number of wood planks in the floor. I tried to sleep. The phantom feeling of a cold gun barrel to my head woke me up almost every time I dozed off. There was no time for dreams. But mainly I cried. This would be the worst Christmas ever.

Trevor tried to come to the door several times over the next few days, but when I heard him pull up in the driveway, I retreated into my bedroom, where I plugged my phone in long enough to text him that I was still alive and wanted to be alone. I'd notice multiple texts and calls from him and others in the brief moments I had my phone on. I just shut off the phone again. It was the same with Emmie when she tried to bring ice cream over. And then there was the deputy who came to check on me. Drew had sent him to do a wellness check. I told him I was fine and to let them know that.

I locked myself in my room and tried to sleep. I had to come to terms with the fact that my relationship with Drew was over, despite being in a place that reminded me of so many happy times we shared. I loved this house. I'd loved our life in it. But he was right. I had told him I wasn't going to watch him destroy himself. As much as I loved him, I had to realize that my love wasn't enough, and as he said, he had to want to fix himself.

And then I thought about Trevor. How could I not? He was kind and thoughtful, and he always seemed to be able to make me laugh – even through the tears. Even though I'd been pushing him away, I really missed being around him. I missed his smile and his sparkling blue eyes. I missed his cooking. But I had to get over Drew, and I didn't know how long that would take. I couldn't shut off my feelings like a faucet. It didn't work that way. Trevor had been a good friend. I wanted to keep that relationship.

I wasn't sure what day it was, but I woke up one day to the sound of pounding on my front door. It was 9 a.m. I never slept that late, ever, but then despair could do that to you. I went to the door to find Jazzy with a beautiful Emmie arrangement.

"This thing is heavy. Cut crystal vases are the absolute heaviest things, and you're making me stand outside with it, Miss Grace."

"Trevor?"

"Yes, ma'am."

"Tell Emmie they're beautiful and she did a wonderful job." That sounded flat, but it was the best I could do.

"Miss Grace, everyone is worried sick about you. And you look terrible."

"Thanks."

"Have you eaten anything?"

"No. I'm not hungry. I just want to be alone."

"And you smell terrible. When's the last time you had a shower?"

"I don't know. I don't even know what day it is. Please leave me alone."

I snapped at her. It wasn't like the Grace I knew. I wasn't sure what was becoming of me. She left; only to return every two hours with another arrangement. This time, they weren't pink roses Trevor was sending me. These were red – the color of love. As she put them down, I counted them because numbers meant something too. Eleven. Not a dozen. There were 11.

"Yes, he knows what the numbers mean," she said. "I told him. I went down the entire list, and he said 11."

Eleven roses mean you're treasured, truly and deeply loved.

From that point, I saw Jazzy every two hours. It was the same delivery – 11 red roses in a cut crystal vase. They were gorgeous.

"Would you please call him?" Jazzy asked after the fourth visit. "I love you, but I'm tired of driving over here. Plus, you're almost out of these vases, and I do not want to have to travel to the mall at Christmas to buy another one for you."

I laughed at her. I loved her straightforwardness. She just spoke her mind.

"I can't."

"Then I will do it for you."

"Battery's dead."

She walked into my room and plugged my phone in.

"I'm sure I'll be back. It's only 3, and we don't close until 6."

"Are there any roses left? Take these back with you and use them if you need them."

"No ma'am. I am under strict orders not to do that. There's a bonus in this for me."

"Oh really? I own the shop."

"What do you always say – the customer is always right? I'm listening to this customer. I'd take a shower if I were you. He's not giving up. Somehow, I think he'll probably show up at some point."

I looked at her. She wrinkled her mouth and narrowed her eyes at me as though she wanted to say something but wasn't sure she should.

"What's wrong, Jazzy?"

"You know it was Dr. Trevor who posted Drew's bond, don't you?"

I felt my mouth drop.

"What are you talking about?"

"Yes, I overheard Miss Emmie and Miss Beth talking, and they said it had to be Dr. Trevor who posted Drew's bond. Who else could do that? You didn't have the money for it, and Beth said she wasn't about to post bond for him even though she could. So, if I were you, I'd take that shower, because he's not taking 'no' for an answer."

I watched her leave.

Could they have been right?

I went into my bedroom and plugged in my phone. Several texts and voice mail messages had been left.

I dialed Drew's number. I was surprised that he actually answered it.

"Grace, everyone has been worried about you."

"Even you?"

"Especially me. This is my fault."

"I still don't understand."

"I know. I'm sorry I've done this to you."

"You didn't have to send a deputy to check on me."

"Yeah, I did. It was for Lottie."

I took a deep breath.

"I just needed to be alone. Drew, I have one question, and I'll leave you alone. Did Trevor post bond for you?"

I heard him take a breath.

"Yeah, yeah, he did. I've been cleared now so there's no danger of him losing his house. The judge cleared me, and I have you to thank for that. And I have thanked Trevor because if he hadn't posted bond, I don't want to think about what would've happened to you."

"I can't remember if I ever thanked you for that."

"Don't. If it hadn't been for me, Gracie, you never would've been in that position in the first place."

I didn't know what to say.

"Have a good day, Drew."

"You too, Grace."

I didn't want to see Trevor, but I did at the same time. If he showed up, I wasn't sure I could push him away again. I took Jazzy's advice and took a shower and washed my hair. And as she predicted around 5 p.m., I heard a car in my driveway and a knock on my door. When I looked out the window, all I could see were the larkspurs - delphinium elatum – royal blue in an arrangement with white roses in a crystal vase. I opened the door.

"I have a delivery for a Ms. Grace Burke Ward," Trevor said as he lowered the flower, so he could see over it. Larkspurs are tall flowers.

"I don't have any place to put them."

He walked in and looked around. I already had four large rose containers. He took the piece into the kitchen.

"I'm sorry for snapping at you the other day and pushing you away. Thank you for remembering my favorite flowers. Where did you get them in December?"

"I have connections, and you're welcome. Everyone has been really worried about you. You don't answer texts or calls, and you've even refused ice cream."

I tried to smile.

"My battery died, and I haven't bothered to charge it."

"I've tried to come by, and you've sent me away. When Emmie said you wouldn't let chocolate chip cookie dough ice cream and sprinkles in, I knew it was serious. At least the flowers got me in the door this time."

"Would you like something to drink?"

"No, Grace, I'm fine. I came to see about you."

I shrugged my shoulders and shook my head. I didn't know what he wanted me to say. I think we all knew I wasn't fine. I was existing, and he was too perfect. My insecurities had snapped into overdrive.

"When's the last time you had anything to eat, Grace?"

"I don't even know what day it is, but the last time I ate anything was with you in Columbia."

"Grace, that was Saturday. Today is Wednesday."

"I'm not hungry."

He went into my kitchen and started to throw open the pantry.

"When's the last time you went to the grocery store?"

"I don't know, but it was before your mom died. There's some cereal in there I think."

He opened the refrigerator and pulled out the milk carton. He looked at the date and walked over to the sink to pour out the soured milk.

"You can't have cereal."

He went back to the refrigerator and pulled open the bins.

"Everything in here is spoiled."

He pulled out his phone.

"Pepperoni?"

"Sure."

"It'll be here in 30 minutes, and I'm staying at least long enough to eat because I'm hungry too. So, I'm not letting you kick me out this time."

"I'm sorry."

"Grace, I think we can let that one slide."

I stood in the archway between the living room and kitchen.

"Cute place."

I smiled.

"I always thought it was. I love this place."

"Would you like to sit on the porch? You seem to like mine.

It's nice out."

"Too many memories on mine."

I turned and walked back into the living room and sat on my couch. I pulled my legs under me. It was my furniture, so I could put my feet on it without hearing my mother's voice telling me to get my feet off the furniture.

He leaned against the arch and put his hands in his jean pockets.

"Take a seat," I said.

He came and sat next to me on the couch, and I pulled a pillow into my lap. Nervous habit. Like a pillow could be a barrier for anything.

"Will you please tell me about what happened this weekend?"

"You said Drew came to see you?"

"Yes, he did."

"Why?"

"He wanted to let me know."

"Then, you know what happened. He's pretty thorough. He does work for the sheriff's department, so he gave you the facts."

I was defensive now. I didn't want to tell Trevor everything. I was all for honesty in relationships, but I felt stupid about how I acted with Drew when he didn't want me anymore.

"I want to hear your side. There are things he doesn't know except for what he heard you say in your statement."

I could hear myself talking, but I sounded so far away. It was just like the statement I gave to Deputy Steed. I was robotic as I related the details of Butch, Jillian, and Drew. I stopped with Drew shooting Jillian.

"All of it, Grace."

His gaze met mine.

"All of what?"

He smiled.

"All of it."

"Which parts do you want to know?" I asked sarcastically.

"Oh, what about the part where Drew told me he left me to protect me from Jillian; then, there's the part where he told me he still loved me, but we just couldn't make things work. Oh, I know, the best part, how one minute I was alone and thinking that if I died my biggest regret would be not being with you and then I threw myself at Drew when he brought me home."

Trevor raised an eyebrow at the last part.

"There, are you happy now?"

I bit my lip, and Trevor didn't respond verbally.

"Are you sure that's all?"

"He brought me home. I didn't have a way to get here. He carried me in because my feet were bandaged. I think I stepped in broken glass when Butch made me walk into the warehouse. We talked."

I paused.

He was staring at me.

"And?"

"He kissed me, and I kissed him back. He said if he'd stayed, things would've gotten complicated. And he was right. They would've, but at the time, I didn't care. I told him that and begged him to stay. He didn't."

Trevor didn't respond right away. I wondered what he was thinking.

"Grace, you and I aren't a couple, are we?"

Did everything have to hurt? I didn't verbally respond, but I know I winced.

"So far, you and I have only been friends – close friends," he continued. "I know you still have feelings for him, and the fact that he saved your life, in a very dramatic fashion, only brought those emotions to the surface again. It's a natural response. He proved that he was your knight in shining armor, and that was something he'd stopped being for you. Now suddenly, he is again; the feelings are there; the timing seems right, but he stopped it because he knew what was taking place. But he never should've kissed you in the first place."

"You're so matter of fact about it."

I pulled the pillow closer.

"Grace, you were married for 10 years. Sunday should've been your 11th anniversary. I know there were a lot of emotions going through you. You told me you had been trying to have a baby for a while. I'm a doctor; I think I know what that means about your relationship with him. And I think that's probably a natural thing to do on your anniversary."

I think I turned red as I glanced away.

"It didn't happen."

"He told me that you were no victim on Sunday."

"Getting out of her hold? It could've been a stupid move. She could've shot me, but she loosened her grip just slightly. I saw an opportunity. I hated her. Trevor, I wanted her dead. She taunted me. She flirted with my – with Drew - in front of me and it made me so mad. Then she told him how stupid I was. I hated her again. She implied that Jazzy was her property. And I hated her all the more. And that bothered me more than you know. I've never hated anyone. I don't even hate Drew."

He reached out for my hand.

"All natural responses. And he let me know that you didn't need to be left alone. He said he didn't stay because he didn't want to send you mixed signals, so I had an idea that something was going on with you."

I stared at him.

"He didn't take advantage."

Again, the raised eyebrow.

"You were vulnerable, and he took advantage of that. How would you feel now if he'd actually stayed and then told you afterward it was a mistake?"

I dragged in a deep breath

"Probably worse."

"Only probably?"

"A lot worse."

"Tell me something, Grace. What did your time alone do for you?"

"What do you mean?"

"Did you work out whatever you needed to? You finally let me in."

"I couldn't say 'no' to four sets of 11 red roses and my delphinium elatum, especially when I know what 11 means," I said and smiled.

"And me?"

I paused. I had one question I needed to ask.

"Why did you post Drew's bond?"

He eyed me suspiciously.

"Did he tell you that?"

"Only after Jazzy told me. I called him and asked. He never would've said anything otherwise."

"I told you I'd lend any resources I could."

"But you put up your parents' house?"

"Well, I didn't do it until after we'd gotten the evidence proving he was set up. A judge has already dismissed his case by the way, so there was no danger of losing the house. Just like you couldn't explain to me why you had to help him, I can't explain to you why I felt compelled to post bond for him. But I'm so grateful I did."

"But still – it's your family home – so many memories."

"There was no danger of losing the house, but I shudder to think what might have happened to you if I hadn't done it. He wouldn't have been there to save you. That house means nothing in comparison."

There was an awkward pause.

"Why did you finally let me in, Grace?" he asked softly.

"I don't want to say 'no' to you. Drew kept telling me it was over. I heard the words, but I didn't listen to them. I kept thinking he would come back. Part of me knew I needed to figure out how to live without him, but he was such a big part of me. I guess I realized that it really is over, and I have to figure out how to get rid of these emotions. I have to start a new life for myself. I want to move forward. And you've been a wonderful friend over the past couple of months."

Just then the doorbell rang. It was the pizza. It was a welcome break. The conversation wasn't as serious for the rest of the evening. He steered it to lighter things. We talked about traveling and all the places we both wanted to go to. We talked about everything and nothing for the next couple of hours. Before my divorce had been final, we did that a lot.

"Grace, I need to go home and get some sleep. I have to drive to Charlotte tomorrow. I have some business to take care of. Don't think that I'm ignoring you; I just probably won't be able to answer my phone."

"So close to Christmas?"

"One of my former patients died."

"I'm so sorry. Must've been a special patient."

"Very special. She didn't die of cancer. She beat cancer multiple times in her life. She was in her 80s. She was one of those people with an indomitable spirit. I loved the life she breathed into people. And she was the one who could sense I wasn't happy. She's the one who told me to go after what I wanted not what someone else told me to want."

"Thanks for coming over. I'm sorry."

"Grace, you've already apologized."

He paused.

"Do you have plans for Christmas Eve?"

"No. I'll be going to my parents' house for Christmas dinner, but I haven't really talked to anyone in the past few days. I haven't made any plans. I've tried not to dwell on the season."

"Would you spend Christmas Eve with me?"

"I'd like that."

"I'll make dinner, but I can't promise a traditional holiday meal."

"Knowing you, whatever you fix will be amazing. It doesn't matter if it's traditional

9

Trevor had been right when he said I wouldn't hear much from him. During my self-imposed exile, I'd missed talking with him. I'd missed seeing the twinkle in his blue eyes, his kind smile, his gentle voice. I had no idea what to get him for a Christmas gift. The shop continued to be busy until Dec. 23, which fell on a Saturday. I didn't feel like braving the mall or any of the shopping centers.

Emmie was still reeling from the fact that she'd been dating a dirty cop, and I wasn't sure what to think about anything. Drew talked about my instinct. I wasn't sure I had anything about Butch. Emmie did, but not until after it was a little late for her. I was ready for this year to be over. It had been too much. But knowing Drew wasn't coming back, I realized I had to move on. I wasn't sure what exactly that meant. After the New Year, I planned to put my house on the market, but I had no idea where I was going to live.

I wasn't sure what to wear on Christmas Eve. Emmie said the holidays were a time to dress up, and that I should. I wasn't sure. I wasn't going to wear Beth's burgundy dress again. I decided on a red velvet, off -the-shoulder shirt with flowing bell sleeves and a black pencil skirt. I put on a pair of black heels. I added some jewelry. I had a ruby choker that went well with the style of the shirt. I stared at myself in the mirror. It should've been like any other time I'd gone to his house, but this time, something felt different. No wedding rings, no Drew to think about. Maybe I was the part of the equation that was different.

He asked me to arrive around 5, and I was right on time. I waited in my car for several minutes and took a deep breath before I headed to the door. I didn't knock, but the door opened. He'd been waiting for me. He was wearing a pair of black trousers and his signature button-up shirt with sleeves rolled to three quarters.

He smiled as he let me in. He didn't say anything for several moments. It wasn't until he'd shut the door behind me that he finally spoke.

"You're simply breathtaking," he said.

"Thank you."

The house smelled wonderful. It was obvious he'd been cooking again. The aroma was familiar. It was his homemade spaghetti sauce.

He led me to what had once been his father's office. It had been one of those rooms hidden behind closed doors for years. I'd only been in the room when I was a teenager, and Trevor had said his mother didn't touch it after his father's death.

The room had three walls of built in bookcases filled with books. One wall had a beautiful carved marble fireplace with a roaring fire. The fourth wall had two floor-to-ceiling windows. The space in between was filled with oil portraits of some of his ancestors.

Most of the furniture had been removed from the room except for a small table, covered with a white linen tablecloth. In two corners of the room, there were massive Christmas trees. And there was a leather couch against the wall with the portraits.

"I brought in the design team of Emmie and Jazzy. I know how much you loved Christmas, and this hasn't been the best Christmas season for you."

I walked over to one of the trees. The room had 12-foot ceilings, and each tree was taller than I was. In my head, I was trying to calculate how many lights were on each tree and how long it would take to decorate them all.

"Mama had so many ornaments," he said, walking over to one

of the trees.   "This one is dedicated to 'The Nutcracker' ballet."

There were tons of miniature nutcrackers in addition to ballerinas and characters from the ballet. I recognized the mouse king and dancers in costumes representing Chinese and Spanish. There were tiny pointe shoes and candy canes. And there were multiple snowflakes.

"Those were her ornaments," he said

I stared at the tree. It told the story of the ballet. I could see the dancers in each scene as I marveled at the ornaments. Several were blown glass; some of the snowflakes were made of crystal. Everything sparkled against the backdrop of the multi-colored lights.

"It's beautiful."

"This one was fun, but it goes in line with 'The Nutcracker' – 'Land of Sweets' and all," he said as he walked to a tree adorned with confectionary ornaments. There were colorful gumdrops, gingerbread cookies, and lollipops. There was a garland made of what looked like hard candies. This tree also had multi-colored lights, hundreds of them.

I touched the tree and its ornaments. I leaned in and closed my eyes as I inhaled the full aroma of the Fraser fir.

"Trevor, this is beautiful."

"Here, let me give you the full effect," he said.

He walked to the other side of the room and turned off the chandelier. The only light came from the hundreds of lights on the trees and the fireplace. I stood there with my mouth open.

Why had he gone to all this trouble?

He walked up behind me.

"Are you hungry?"

"Yes."

"Then, come over here and have a seat."

He pulled out the chair for me, and I waited. He pushed the food in on a cart and left it at the door.

"When did you have time to do all of this?"

"I didn't have much to do with it. Jazzy and Emmie were kind enough to come and decorate in the evenings while I was gone."

"They did a fantastic job of keeping a secret."

He smiled.

The first course was a salad – the same strawberry and feta cheese with champagne vinaigrette that we'd had on the day that we learned about the video footage that freed Drew.

"Sparkling grape juice for the lady," he said, pouring it into a cut-crystal glass. He also poured the non-alcoholic beverage into his own glass instead of the red wine he'd had before.

He noticed me staring at him and smiled at me.

"Drew's drinking tore the two of you apart. I'm not Drew, and I'll do everything I can to prove that to you."

I took a deep breath and fidgeted in the chair. I tried to sit up straight, and I couldn't decide how to sit. Legs crossed at the ankles?

He stared at me.

"Why are you so nervous, Grace?"

"I'm not nervous."

He smiled and winked at me.

"Your breathing is more rapid than usual, and your hands are slightly trembling. And you are a horrible liar."

I swallowed hard and didn't reply.

"It's just me, Grace. I haven't changed."

"Everything is different, and you know it."

"Really?" he grinned.

"Why did you do this for me?"

"Because I wanted to make tonight special."

"Why?"

"I wanted to give you some of the joy that you give to other people. December should be a month of joy, and it's been anything but that for you. I know how much you love Christmas."

"Okay."

"Are you finished with your salad?"

I started to stand up to move the plate.

"No, Grace. I invited you."

He replaced the plates with the spaghetti. Instantly, my brain flashed back to the night when I'd first delivered flowers to his mother. Drew had just left me a few days before. Trevor had made spaghetti and asked me to eat with him. Later that night, Drew accused me of having an affair with him. And I foolishly said that we only ate spaghetti. It wasn't a big deal. I'd told Trevor that, and he laughed.

I stared at him.

"Spaghetti can be very romantic," he said. He knew what I was thinking.

I smiled at him.

"You're right."

It was romantic in the glow of lights from the Christmas trees.

"How was your trip?"

He smiled.

"Changing the subject?"

"Well, I did want to know."

"It was good. I met with a real estate agent, and we put my condo on the market. I made my final goodbyes at the practice I was part of, signed lots of documents. And I attended a beautiful memorial service."

"So, you're moving back here?"

"It's a huge possibility. There will be an opening at the medical college, teaching students. One of the professors is retiring. This house is mine. My brothers have homes of their own, and it was my mother's wish for me to get the house. They are fine with it. The only stipulation is that if I choose to sell it, the proceeds are split four ways."

"You're so good with people. I saw you with Miss Millie. How is she, by the way?"

"There was a lump on the side of her neck. It was removed. It was benign, and she loves my brother."

"I'm glad to hear that."

"There's a ministry downtown – doctors providing medical

care of for the uninsured and underinsured. I've talked to them about possibly helping there some."

"Sounds like you have a plan."

He winked at me.

"A partial one. I'm hazy on some things."

Dessert was amazing. It was a chocolate cheesecake.

"You are an incredible chef. Thank you."

After we'd finished the meal, he moved to the couch against the wall.

"Come and sit with me," he said, motioning to the spot next to him. "And don't worry about the dishes. You seem to forget that I've lived on my own for a long time with no one to clean up after me."

"No, I was always taught that you offer your help in situations like this."

"And I was taught the same thing."

I nervously moved to the couch with him. I took a deep breath.

"Emmie told me that you asked her what was wrong with you," he said softly.

"Emmie needs to learn to keep her mouth shut."

"Possibly. But Grace, there's nothing wrong with you."

I glanced away, trying to blink back those stupid tears.

"Two men have left me. Something must be wrong with me."

He touched my cheek brushing the tears away. Then, he grasped my hand in his.

"No, there was something wrong with him and me, but I learned my lesson."

I gazed into his eyes for several moments. He leaned forward and gently kissed me. I didn't want to fight this. All the feelings came rushing to the surface. I was swept back into being a teenager. I remembered the first time Trevor kissed me. He was my first kiss. It was one of those awkward moments where his face planted against mine. It was during a high school football game and our team had scored a touchdown. In the excitement, he hugged me and kissed me. I remembered other times, and then I remembered Drew and the last time he'd kissed me before he left me. I wasn't sure how long the kiss lasted. How did 17 years of your life just go by in a flash? He touched my face as he released me.

"There's nothing wrong with you," he whispered. "Absolutely nothing."

I didn't say anything.

"I need to make a confession," he said.

I wasn't sure what to make of that. What kind of confession?

"Before I make my confession, I need to back up a few years."

"Okay."

"I was forced into breaking up with you," he started.

"We established that."

"I had nothing. I knew nothing. I should've been more of a man, but I was still a kid."

"I don't hold it against you. You've already explained and apologized."

"And I've hated myself every single day since I let my father bully me into kicking you out of my life. And I haven't forgiven myself for hurting you."

I glanced down at my hand which was intertwined with his.

"It wasn't what I wanted. We broke up Christmas break of my sophomore year although I knew at the beginning of the school year, I had to do it. I thought that I could keep it a secret – from them, from him. But they found out so there was a big confrontation right before we broke up. After I broke your heart, I threw myself into school. My mother knew I was miserable. I didn't come home at spring break. During the summer, I stayed with my college roommate and his family near Atlanta. Mama begged me to come home. And I told her why I couldn't."

He paused and glanced away.

"I broke her heart several times too," he took a deep breath. "If I had come home, I would've wanted to see you, but I didn't want

169

to hurt you. I tried to forget you. I joined a fraternity, but I hated it. I joined an intramural cross-country club. I ran a lot, and I dated a lot of girls, hoping to forget you."

He took my hand and gently rubbed his thumb across my fingers. He gazed into my eyes.

"During my junior year, I went with my parents to the beach during spring break, and my mother told me that I needed to go to you. Maybe I could make things right between us. When we got back from Hilton Head, I went to your house, but there were several girls there. I think Emmie was there. I just couldn't, and I missed my chance," he said.

He paused again and shook his head.

"I'll never forgive myself for that. The next time I came home was summer break. I went to your house, and your mother kindly told me that you'd just started dating Drew Ward. She said you were so happy. When she asked me if I wanted her to tell you I'd stop by, I told her 'no.'"

He touched my cheek.

"That night I came home and informed my father I would not be applying to the Medical College, I would apply anywhere but Augusta. And if he didn't like it, well, let's just say I only wish I'd done that two years before, because he backed down some."

Another pause.

"I ended up in Charleston at medical school there. I loved being near the beach. It was healing. I even met someone at medical school. We dated for about a year. When it came time to graduate, she took a residency in Washington state, and I went to Charlotte. I didn't want to leave the South. I skipped Augusta as much as I could. Every time I came home, Mama would apologize for what had happened. She begged me to believe it wasn't her. And I did. I didn't come home much because it limited the possibility of me running into you."

He shrugged his shoulders.

"There's the backstory so to speak. Two months before Bill

died, Mama was diagnosed with cancer. She'd had cancer before so when it recurred, it wasn't good. You remember that Dana came on the weekends to see Mama, and Dana's mama, Mary Louise, is good friends with your mama?"

"Yes, Augusta is a small place."

"One Saturday, Dana came with her arms loaded. This time she brought her mother. They came with a beautiful flower arrangement made by a certain Grace Ward, and your mom's incredible lemon pound cake or whatever it's called. I helped them in, and Mama asked lots of questions about your family. She always loved you. It was just a natural segue. I usually didn't listen to the gossip, but this was one day I was a fly on the wall. It came up in the conversation that you hadn't seen Dana in months and you'd never met Lily. And apparently, according to Miss Mary Louise, Miss Lottie had told her that you and Drew weren't doing well. Your marriage was in trouble and had been for months. She even said you'd left him at one point and were trying to patch things together. It was like putting "a piece of duct tape on the Titanic" from what Mary Louise said. You were the subject of several minutes of gossip, I'm afraid.".

"Apparently, I'm good at giving people something to talk about. How did I not know things were so bad, but everyone else seemed to?"

He smiled.

"You have an optimism, Grace, that few people have. Anyway, Dana gave me several glances during the conversation. I couldn't tell what she was thinking, but she had known that I had dated you. We talked once on one of my breezes through Augusta. I never had an affair with her, by the way."

"I never believed you did especially when I asked you about it. You acted like I'd asked if you kissed your sister. But this is a fascinating story go on."

"Well, I told you I wasn't perfect so here goes."

He stopped and took a breath.

"After that visit, Dana made it a point to tell me that you'd be

171

doing the flowers for Bill's soiree. And I came and watched that night. I wasn't there to support Bill."

"Emmie told me she saw you watching me. I didn't see you."

"No. You were too busy trying to placate Drew and Bill. And you also didn't want to attract any attention from anyone. You did a great job hiding in the shadows. I could tell you were uncomfortable. I could also tell that things between you and Drew weren't good. Your body language said a lot. You folded your arms whenever he spoke to you; you glanced away. You didn't look him in the eye often. You just looked sad. Emmie tried to cheer you up."

I didn't want to talk about that night.

"So, are we getting closer to this confession?"

"Very. When I said I came to see you in your shop to clear the air, that was true. When I told you that I wanted my mother to have lots of flowers while she was living, that was the truth. That arrangement Dana had brought was the spark to that idea. Mama lit up when she saw it. And the part about me wanting to take control of my own life was also the truth. All the regrets – I was and still am filled with them."

"Okay? I don't understand your confession."

"Those are partial truths. The rest of the truth is I wanted to see if you still had feelings for me. You were suspicious of my timing, and you should've been. You'd asked about the timing of everything, and yes, I'd planned it that way. Apparently, I planned it better than I realized because I didn't know he'd walked out the night before I showed up. You looked rough that morning, but the way you looked didn't matter. Despite the dark circles from obviously being awake for several days and crying, you were the most beautiful thing I'd seen in a long time. From the things I had heard from Dana and others over the years, I knew that you'd turned into the woman I always thought you'd be."

"What are you talking about?"

"You have always been a champion for the underdog. You could've been in the popular crowd, but you chose to be friends with the Goth queen Emmie and her black lips, black fingernails and spiked collars."

I laughed.

"Wow, she is so far from that now."

He smiled back.

"And Beth wore glasses, carried an extra 50 pounds and wore braces."

"I'd forgotten about that. Definitely a swan underneath that ugly duckling, but we were all friends when we were 6. We just stuck together despite our differences. I've always thought they were beautiful, so it never occurred to me."

"You cared, Grace. You always did. It didn't matter what anyone looked like, even though other people can be so superficial in high school. That's what set you apart. You volunteered at the food bank and did community service. You went the extra mile. But you always stayed in the background. And now, look at you. You and your outcast friends have taken in a woman off the streets and are trying to help her get an education. You've given her a job and meaning. She has a place to live, and you've given her friends that care about her."

I nodded.

"Now, you're trying to make me sound perfect."

"No, Grace, I'm just trying to tell you why I could never forget you and why I looked at every other woman through you. And you're smart. You own a business. You brought your talented friends in and are making this work."

I swallowed hard.

"So, I went to your shop the Monday after Bill died. I needed to see you. I was so nervous about it. You could've been angry; maybe you should've been. I was willing to risk it," he paused. "I couldn't exactly say I was there to see if there was the smallest possibility of a second chance, now could I?"

"No. I would've told you 'no.'"

"I know you would've. You've uttered that word several times, but I wanted to see if there was some glimmer there. Anything."

He smiled.

"When you saw me, after the shock faded, you had a look I can't describe. It was a mix of joy and sorrow. You seemed happy to see me but sad at the same time. I hoped the sadness was the same as the sadness I'd felt. When I told you that you were beautiful, you smiled and blushed. Who does that? But you did. It was then that I knew there was still something there. It might have been buried, but it was still there. And I kept watching through every encounter with you. And part of me came to your shop that day because I wanted to see if I could find out just how bad things were for you. Word got back to me quickly that Drew had left you. Dana called me. She'd told me that you'd given him an ultimatum in the spring, and he hadn't completely lived up to his part of the deal. She told me about his addiction." '

"Why?"

"Because she saw in Drew some of the same things, she saw in Bill."

I took a deep breath.

"I deliberately had you deliver those flowers to us that night, a week after Bill died. I had dinner ready. I begged you to stay. And trust me, I could've made that dinner so much more romantic than it was. And that was the reason for tonight's menu. To prove to you that spaghetti can be very romantic," he smiled and winked at me. "I told you my partial story, and I know you reluctantly told me what was going on in your life that night. I also know that when I asked you what you were afraid of, you were afraid of how you were feeling about me. You were afraid of those feelings stirring inside you. I was so close to taking you into my arms and kissing you. The night would've ended very differently if I had."

I glanced down.

"What if things had worked out between Drew and me?"

"Then, I probably would be moving to Charleston about now, but they didn't."

He paused and searched my face.

"Anyway, if I drove a nail into the coffin of your marriage, I'm not sorry. Not in the least bit. And I won't apologize for it."

I drew in a deep breath and stared at him. I wasn't sure what to say, or what kind of response he expected. I guess it had been obvious to everyone but me that my marriage had been in serious trouble for a while. I knew we were having problems, but I always thought they'd work out somehow. I always thought Drew would come around and get help. I never thought he'd leave, and I still didn't want to admit it was over.

"If you don't want to talk to me after this, I understand, but know that I want to be with you more than anything."

He brushed my cheek with the tips of his fingers and seemed to be waiting for a response. His confession surprised me a little, but probably not as much as he thought. I had never believed in coincidences.

"So, you're telling me I was right."

I smiled.

"Yes, your instincts are right about a lot of things. You knew I was holding something back. You didn't completely believe my partial truths."

"Were you trying to manipulate me?"

"Was I? Possibly. But, you were smart enough to question my motives. You knew what was going on. You weren't going to let me do that. You didn't have to deliver those flowers and visit with us. You could've gotten Jazzy to deliver them. You didn't have to do it personally. You didn't have to linger. You didn't have to keep coming over. I think you even made flowers I didn't order, and I know you didn't charge them to my card."

"No, you didn't manipulate me. I wanted to be near you. You cared about me even with everything you were going through with your mom. You were kind, and when everything around me was falling apart, you somehow needed me. That gave me a reason to go on when my main reason was gone."

"I relied on your emotional support, and I probably shouldn't

175

have done that because I knew you were dealing with Drew and all the pain he was causing you. But it hurt me that you shut me out from the divorce process. It wasn't like I didn't ask you, but every time I did, you pushed me away."

"I said this before. Your mother was dying. I watched her die too, remember? How could I tell you about my own problems when I watched the agony Miss Harper was going through? She tried to smile; she tried to be joyful. She was amazing, but I knew she was trying to be strong for you and your brothers. A divorce was nothing compared to watching your mother die. Besides, being there for you and her made me feel needed, and that's a big part of who I am. I need to feel needed. I need to have purpose. The person who once needed me the most didn't want or need me anymore. I felt my purpose had slipped away. Focusing on you and your family helped me. I could channel my energy somewhere besides feeling sorry for myself."

"But that's only half the truth, and you know it."

I glanced away. He was right. I had put up all sorts of barriers. I could give to Trevor and his family, but I didn't want them to try to give back to me or to let them in. I let his mother in. I was afraid of letting him in completely.

"I figured if I kept you in the dark about my divorce, then I wouldn't have to talk about the emotions I felt where you were concerned, and you wouldn't bring up a relationship with us."

"And I knew that. Funny that we can't seem to keep secrets from each other, isn't it?"

"Yeah. That's true. I've heard everything you've said, but I don't know how to get past this fear of screwing everything up again. I'm still in love with Drew."

"I know that, Grace, but you never got over me either."

I glanced away. He was right. I never had gotten over my first love.

"I still need you, Grace. I need you in my life. I didn't realize how much until you shut me out last weekend. Not being able to talk to you or see you or watch you bring flowers to my house was one of the hardest things I've gone through. I realized how empty my life now was."

He smiled at me and touched my cheek.

"I'm not asking you to marry me or move in with me. I'm not even asking you to spend the night with me," he whispered. "I'm only asking one thing."

"What's that?"

"You were willing to give Drew dozens of second chances. Just give me one chance. That's all I'm asking is for one chance that I'll take every day for the rest of my life to prove to you that you made the right decision. I'm in love with you, Grace."

I was surprised to hear those words. I'm not sure why because deep down I knew it. I just stared at him. I reached out and touched his cheek. I didn't know how to respond at first.

"I'm willing to give you – us – another chance, but I need things to go slowly, really slowly."

"I've waited 15 years," he said and kissed my hand. "We can go at a snail's pace."

www.ingramcontent.com/pod-product-compliance
Lightning Source LLC
Chambersburg PA
CBHW020650260626
47157CB00008B/2978